The Zinnia Tales

On behalf of all the writers, enjoy!

Timmy Robinson Smith

Mountain Girl Press
Bristol, Virginia

This is a work of fiction. Any resemblance to actual persons, either living or dead is entirely coincidental. All names, characters, and events are the product of the author's imagination. Any resemblance to persons, living or dead is purely coincidental.

The Zinnia Tales

Mountain Girl Press
Published September 2006

Cover design by
Big Dawg Design, Bristol, Tennessee

You may contact the publisher at:
Mountain Girl Press
P.O. Box 17013
Bristol, VA 24209-7013
E-mail: publisher@mountaingirlpress.com

ISBN: 978-0-9767793-1-5

Contents

Introduction

The Zinnia Tales, an anthology of Appalachian stories from Mountain Girl Press, is delightful and touching.

In the lead story, *The Zinnia Tales*, author Tammy Robinson Smith takes a tender look at family relationships. *Road Trip to Albany*, by Pam Keaton, traces a journey of discovery that leads to a sense of belonging. *Cooking for the Dead*, by Jennifer Mullins, reveals real thoughts and secrets as neighborhood women prepare to say goodbye to one of their own.

In *Party Line*, Lisa Hall tells about neighbors who keep their fingers on the pulse of Fletcher Hollow, and prove after a mine accident that phone conversations are not the only ties that bind them together. In *Blackberry Spring*, Kori Frazier takes a grim look at coal country and how the mine owners prey upon those who work there and their families. In *Secrets in the Cedar Chest* by Susan Harmon, Molly discovers part of her family's past and maybe meets her future while snowbound in her grandmother's cabin.

In *Mad Dogs*, by author P. J. Wilson, as a young girl's brother flits in and out of her life, she learns that her only salvation is within herself. *Gracie's Cabin*, written by Susanna Holstein, tells the story of Annie Rose's friendship with a strange woman in the woods, which leads her down a path of no return. *Key to a Door*, by Mary McMillan Terry is a story about giving change a chance as tall, insecure Sarah discovers that home may be where you make it. In *The Day the Devil Beat His Wife*, by Tricia Scott, Ginny loses her husband to a trusted friend, but gains insight as she recalls a past where her imagination offered a welcome escape.

Cleo has a husband who never ceases to exasperate her with his home repair mishaps in *She Married a Bonehead* by Tammy Wilson. Mothers always think their child is beautiful, but this mother gets surprising verification from an unexpected source, in *The True Beauty* by Rebecca Williams. In *Burning the Trash*, by Susanna Holstein, Emma thought she'd made the right choice about her estate, but soon discovers she needs to rethink her bequest. Sometimes we envy what we don't have, only to find out, as Laura and Rachel do in *Fine Ways* by Donna Akers Warmuth, that all is not as it seems. Welcome to *Jewel Holler*, written by Tammy Robinson Smith, where coming home has extra meaning to one of three sisters.

This is a book well worth reading and I would recommend it highly. A wonderful collection of heart-warming stories!

Carol Guy
Co-author of *Vengeance Can Wait*

Foreword

Some projects begin just like faith, with the planting of a tiny mustard seed; or in this case, the planting of a zinnia bed. It is my greatest wish that the stories you are about to read will plant the seeds of joy, hope, and love in your life; just as those seeds were planted for the sisterhood of women characters in this collection of stories.

Although these stories are fiction, the women they portray are as real as your mother, grandmother, sister, aunt, niece or best friend. We all know these characters; we need only to look at the people whom we hold dear to find them.

For me, the writers of these stories have become as special to me, as their characters are to them. Each writer had something unique to say, and each one did it so well with her words and characterizations. I owe them a debt of gratitude for sharing their work for this story collection.

I must mention one very important woman who helped get this book to press; Sally Crockett, editor and proofreader extraordinaire. Thanks for your input, your insight and your part in making this book one of which we can all be proud.

And thanks to all of the people who continue to support the work of Mountain Girl Press. Your contributions are never unnoticed and are always appreciated.

Tammy Robinson Smith
Publisher
Mountain Girl Press

For all the mountain girls . . .

Tammy Robinson Smith

The Zinnia Tales

The Grandmother

I am just so fed up with him and his sinful readin'. Mama would have his hide if she knew he was bringin' that filth in the house—and on top of everything else, for him to get mad at me. Does he think I deserve to be treated this a' way?

* * * * *

I run up the bank from the bottom of the hill. I've been plannin' on plantin' my zinnies for two days, but what with all the cleanin' at the house, and cookin' for the saw mill hands, it seems to me like I never git a free minute to do what I want. I guess that's just the way it is, now that I'm a married woman. But, by golly, he can just do without his supper if he thinks I'm goin' to put up with him and his worldly ways. A perfectly good Bible sittin' there on the table, and he's out paying hard earned money to buy *True Detective Stories* to read.

Oh, I am just so mad I could spit!

I'm gittin' my zinny bed planted right now. That's it. I'll stay out here all night if I have to. I kneel down on the warm ground. I look all around me at the signs of spring. The grass is starting to green up. The crocuses and daffodils put on quite a show for Easter this year.

I'll tell you one thing. Andrew won't live to see next Easter, if he ever does again, what he did to me today.

1

I stand up and grab the pick I left a layin' here yesterday when I was measurin' for my zinny bed. Andrew would probably fuss about that too, if he found out I left his tool here a layin' on the ground. Least the dew wasn't bad enough to make it rust. I start to work . . . and think.

* * * * *

I still can't believe what happened earlier this afternoon. I'd been workin' since sunup this morning. I hung out six loads of washin' before ten o'clock, and still had dinner on the table for the mill hands at noon. I had just got the dinner mess cleaned up when Andrew came in from the mill to do his bookwork. I still had washin' to gather in, and was goin' to start supper; and there he come in and plopped down on a kitchen chair. Then, he propped his feet on the table, just like he didn't have a bit of raisin'.

I knew then my temper would git the best of me. Mama always told me it would be my undoin' some day. I know that now that I'm a married woman I'm supposed to listen to my husband and give him the comforts he needs; but I tell you, I haven't lived seventeen years without learnin' a few things. Why, it's just not good manners to put your feet on the table like that. Then, to take that magazine out, and start readin' it right in front of me. Least he could of taken it outside, and looked at it in the shed. It's hard tellin' what kind of talk they put in that kind of book. *True Detective Stories* indeed!! I bet not one of 'em is true.

The tears start to spill out of my eyes as I think about the terrible fuss me and Andrew had over that book. I am just so tired. I have worked myself to death today. Seein' him sitting there, while I still had so much to do, and knowin' that he thought it was all right to sit and read blasphemy, while I's a workin'—why, it was just more than I could stand!

So, I grabbed the book out of his hand . . .

It was what happened next that makes the tears flow even harder when I think about it now. When I grabbed the magazine it caught Andrew unaware. He started hollerin' as his chair fell backward, then he jumped forward and tumbled onto the kitchen floor. I could tell by the look on his face, when he got stood up, that he was mad as could be that I'd grabbed his book from him that way.

But, why oh why, did he have to go and slap my face?

I can't believe my sweet Andrew did something like that to me. If my mama only knew. But I can't go cryin' to her like a child. She'd just tell me I've made my bed, and now I'll just have to lay in it.

It just hurts my soul. My Andrew ain't never done nothin' like that to me; or for that matter, he ain't never done nothin' like that to nobody – why, it's shameful to think he could.

* * * * *

Whew! I've broken up enough ground for three rows of plantin' since I've been out here. The feel of the pick stabbin' the ground is good, after all the anger I've been feelin' inside of me. I guess I better see about layin' off the rows first; that's the way Mama always goes about fixin' her zinny bed. I'm not real sure how to go about plantin' this zinny bed, but I think I'm smart enough to figure it out.

"Eliza."

I turn around and look straight into Andrew's eyes.

"What do you want?"

I hope he didn't come up here to start fussin' at me. I'm just not in the mood to keep at it.

"Eliza, I got something for you . . . I hope you like it."

Andrew hands me a flower vase. It's black, and smooth and simple, but really pretty.

"Eliza," Andrew continues, "I don't know what come over me. There's not any excuse for actin' the way I did. I don't know how I could have lost my fool head like that. I left the house after you did, and went walkin' up on the back forty for a little

3

while. I've been up there most of the afternoon. You know that old shed up there?"

I nod.

"Well, I got to pokin' around in there, and come to find out, there's a lot of old stuff packed away in some wooden crates. I found this here vase, and there's some tools and iron pots and stuff. Maybe we could go up there together sometime, and look through it. I thought about the flowers you've been talkin' about, and when I saw this here vase – well, I thought maybe you'd like it. That's all . . . I reckon I orta git back down to the house now."

Andrew turns to walk back down the hill. I know I ort to be madder than I am now, but somehow I know he's tryin' hard to let me know he done wrong. I guess maybe I can forgive him . . . this one time.

"Andrew," I yell to his retreating back, "Come on back up here, and help me git this flower bed dug up. I've been up since before daylight, and I'm a gittin' mighty tired!"

"What . . . what the devil?"

Andrew looks shocked that I've ordered him to come up the hill; but he just might want to get used to it.

"Yes, you heard me. I said you need to git up here and help me, if you want me to have fresh flowers to put in that vase come summertime."

I think I'm gittin' his attention now!

"Well, you're mighty feisty for a slip of a girl, I tell you now."

Andrew is startin' to laugh . . . and you know I may just start laughin' too!

The Mother

It's getting dark outside. I don't like the dark. I wish everybody would just go on home, and leave Mommy alone. I know the doctor could make her better if everybody would just get out of his way. Mommy used to feel better after the doctor would

4

come and give her shots. Jane and Edina must not be doing it right. Ever since they started giving Mommy her shots, she's just been getting sicker and sicker.

Maybe I can peep around the corner and see what's going on in there. There's Mrs. Morefield from church; she's Mommy's friend. She's holding Mommy's hand just like Mommy holds mine when I'm sick. The preacher just keeps going on and on talking about Heaven. I wish he would just be quiet. Daddy always says we need to be quiet so Mommy can rest.

I slip past the bedroom real quiet and make my way out to the porch through the front door. There's even more people out here. I'll just sit here on the glider, and maybe they'll all go away. I wish they would leave us alone.

* * * * *

I'm so cold. I sit up and rub my arms. Where am I, and who is that I hear crying? My eyes adjust to the soft darkness which has crept down around our house while I lay sleeping on the glider. The crying is getting louder, and it sounds like my Daddy. But that can't be, my Daddy is a big grownup man; I know he wouldn't cry.

I get up and creep slowly to the front door, wanting to know what's going on, but I feel so funny in my stomach. I'm not sick like Mommy, just scared like when my brothers lock me inside the outhouse, and won't let me out. I look inside and see my Daddy. He's holding Mommy to his chest. Everyone's just standing around watching him, and looking sad.

"Eliza, oh my Eliza," Daddy is crying so loud, and I'm so scared.

I open the door wider and run into the room.

"My little girl," Daddy cries as he lets loose of Mommy and grabs me real tight, "your Mommy just went to Heaven."

"Hush, Andrew, let that child go," Mrs. Morefield says as she pulls me from Daddy.

"No, I don't want you; I want my Daddy; I want my Mommy," I am getting really upset with her.

5

Why won't they leave us alone? I just want them all to go away.

"Hush, child, now you run along and go down to Edina's," Mrs. Morefield says, ushering me out of the room.

I go out the front door and I start running, but I'm not going down to Edina's. I run as fast as I can, by the porch and up the hill. I'm going to Mommy's flowerbed.

* * * * *

I fling myself onto the ground beside her flowerbed. Mommy didn't get to plant her zinnies this year. Daddy had to do it for her because she was so sick. I remember the day he planted the seeds. I sat on Mommy's bed and talked to her. We could almost see Daddy out the bedroom window; but the hill is real high; and Daddy was real far away.

She told me the story of her zinny vase that day. I didn't understand all of it. I think Daddy gave her the vase after he did something that made her mad. Sometimes Mommy gets mad; but most of the time she's happy; that is she was, until she got sick. I wish these zinnies would bloom. Daddy told Mommy she'd see them bloom this year. It looks like to me some of them should open up soon.

I get real close to the flowers and through the darkness try to find one that's blooming . . . but it's just so hard to see when it's nighttime on a lonely hillside, you're only eleven years old, you've got tears pouring out of your eyes and deep down inside, you know your Mommy's not going to see her flowers bloom this year.

The Granddaughter

"Cady, grab the trowel there, the metal one, not that cheap plastic one."

"Okay, just give me a second. Mom, you guys have more junk than anyone I know. I hope you're not going to rely on me to sort through this mess when you're dead and gone."

"When I'm dead and gone, do you think I'm going to rely on you for anything?"

"Good point."

* * * * *

Every year I come to my mom's house to help her plant her zinnias. We've been doing this together since I was a little girl. It's a task I enjoy deep down inside, but I would die before I would let my mom know just how much I enjoy it. Telling her I enjoy it would mean letting go of the small vestige of power I think I have over my mother. If she ever discovers the depth of my sentimentality over the zinnia bed, my goose is cooked. She'll know I'm a marshmallow and not the unwilling draftee I try to make her think I am.

This year is different though. I didn't come home to plant the zinnias . . . I was already here.

* * * * *

"Cady, I left the zinnia seeds in the house on the kitchen counter. Run in there and get them."

"Yes, Mother," I said, doing a fair impression of a curmudgeon.

I'm beginning to wonder where I learned that word. I'm using it a lot lately.

I go inside to get the seeds, smiling as I see the plain, black vase on the fireplace mantel. It sits there faithfully waiting, each year; until my mom's zinnias bloom, and it is filled again with the colorful blossoms. As I stroll back out to the garden it hits me that I am feeling the first stirrings of something akin to joy . . . an emotion I haven't experienced very much of lately.

However, the signs of springtime do that to me. They remind me why this is my favorite time of year. Springtime makes me happy as I watch the crocuses begin to push their heads up through the ground. When the first buds start popping out on the dogwood trees, I know the world will soon be colored with their blossoms. Leaving behind the gray shades of winter makes me feel more alive and energetic. And, of course, it means helping my mother plant her flowers.

"Your dad had Clarence till this soil last week. I hope we're not rushing the season. Mommy always said to wait until after the tenth of May to plant flowers, but I think we've had our last frost."

Mom surveys the area that is ready for planting as she slips off her sweater. She kneels down beside the bed and begins sifting through the pan of seeds I brought to her.

I always smile inside when my sixty-seven year old mother refers to her mother as Mommy. I guess it has something to do with my grandmother dying when my mom was only eleven. It's a term of endearment for the mother she didn't get a chance to know as an adult. Yet, it is such a paradox to hear someone with laugh lines and gray hair talk about her Mommy.

"I think we've had the last frost this year, Mom. It's been seventy degrees every day since last week," I say, crouching down beside her.

"Where did you get these seeds? Did Aunt Jane give them to you?" I ask.

"No," Mom says apprehensively, "They came from your flowerbed."

"My flowerbed, what do you mean? In case you haven't noticed, I don't have a flowerbed anymore, much less a yard, or a house for that matter."

For some reason I am getting a little testy.

"They came from the house on Goodacre Road."

"Oh."

"Your flowers bloomed after you all moved up north last year. They were so pretty. I picked some of your zinnias to save for seed before the new owners moved in."

"I didn't know. I mean I remember you said they bloomed. I think I told you just not to tell me about it. I didn't want to know that someone else was enjoying the flowers

8

I planted. Do you know that's the first time I had ever planted zinnias for myself? Before, I always came here to help you. I guess it just wasn't meant for me to have a zinnia bed of my own."

I know it doesn't seem like a big deal, but it is for me, especially this year.

"Did I ever tell you about the year Daddy planted the zinnias for Mommy?"

My mom deftly changes the subject.

"No."

"It was the spring that she was really sick. He dug up the bank out by the side of the front porch of the home place. He planted that whole hillside with zinnias. When he finished planting the seeds, he got her out of bed, and helped her to the front porch. He showed her where the zinnias would bloom that year. Mommy told him she wouldn't be around when the zinnias bloomed. He wouldn't listen to her though. He said, 'Oh yes, you'll be here when the zinnias bloom, Eliza.' But she wasn't."

"She didn't see the flowers he planted for her?"

"No, but she was there when the zinnias bloomed. The morning of her funeral, the hillside just exploded with zinnia blooms. Daddy went out and picked three or four, in different shades of peach to match her dress. He brought them inside to place in her hand and he said to her, 'See Eliza, I told you that you would be here when the zinnias bloomed.' I don't think he ever stopped grieving for her fully. He loved her so much. You know, Cady, that's the way a husband should love his wife."

"I know, Momma, oh, how I know."

Silence envelops us as I watch my mother plant the seeds that came from my flowerbed. I think about the fact that I didn't get to see my zinnias bloom; but then again, neither did my grandmother. For several months I have been trying to cope with the fact that I will be raising my son alone. That thought is terrifying to me; but I can't imagine how my grandmother felt all those years ago, realizing she wasn't even going to be around to raise her children. She left such a legacy, though. For instance, here I am, a granddaughter she never met, planting zinnias with my mother and trying to heal myself. Maybe planting zinnias has an emotional healing value that I can reap come summertime.

"Cady, are you listening?"

"Sorry, Mother. What did you say?"

"I said you could do more than watch me work."

"Yes, but it wouldn't be near as much fun for me."

The look of indignation on her face makes it worth hearing the martyred sigh of resignation that inevitably follows, and always gets on my nerves. However, obeying my better instincts, I start poking small holes into the dirt, at reasonably ordered six-to-eight inch intervals. I then begin dropping the flower seeds into the holes I've made.

"You know, Momma, I can't even remember the first time I helped you do this."

"I can. The first time you actually helped was when you were four years old. It was the summer after you had been in the hospital for that awful stomach virus. You were still so pale and skinny, but you wanted to come out with me to the `zinny' bed. You always said 'zinny' when you were little. I thought that was so sweet because that's what Mommy called zinnias too. It must have been how her mother pronounced zinnia. Of course, you didn't know any better, and she didn't know any different. But it was a connection for me. I thought maybe she was playing a little game with me, through you."

An introspective look comes across my mom's face as she reaches for another handful of seeds. When I was growing up, she always told me that she felt her mother knew what was going on in her life. She said she felt her mom watched her in piano recitals; saw her on her wedding day, and the days each of us was born. Part of me wants to believe that too, but part of me is just so jaded by my life that I think it's just her way of compensating for the absence of a maternal figure in her life. Some-times I wish I could be more like Peter Pan and just believe.

"You know I wouldn't have believed it when we came out here, but I think you may be enjoying yourself."

My mom's words snap me out of my reverie.

"Well, don't get to used to it. This is too much like real work," I retort quickly, getting in the last word . . . for once.

* * * * *

Later that evening I go out onto the front porch to "porch sit" for awhile. That's what we call it when we sit on the iron furniture that used to grace the front porch of my grandparents' home. It's been painted every color of the rainbow; and when the most recent coat begins to peel, you can see the ghosts of colors past. It's comforting when I think about my mom describ-ing to me the times she remembers her mother sitting on this furniture, after supper, trying to catch a moment's rest before finishing up her work for the evening. Or listening to her describe the nights after her mother's death, when her daddy would sit in the glider with her until the wee hours. Somehow it must have brought comfort to both of them being where the woman they loved so much had spent so many peaceful moments. Our front porch, just like my grandparents', is a good place to think.

Slam.

Well, sometimes it's a good place to think.

The side door falls shut as my mother makes her escape from the house. Deep down in my heart, I knew trying to catch a moment's peace was asking for too much at this house.

"Do you know what your father did just now?"

My mother takes her place on the one chair that has a pillow on the seat. I've never asked her why she has to have a pillow on her seat. I'm pretty sure it's got something to do with a malady that I don't want to discuss.

"Your father," my mother continues, oblivious to my indifference, "took Jonah out to the flower bed so he could watch him sprinkle Sevin dust on it. He'll kill those flowers before they ever have a chance to grow. I'd like to know what makes him so obsessed with putting that stuff on all green things. You would think he could find better things to do than mess in my flowers."

"Maybe he secretly wants to sabotage your zinnias," I say, knowing full well that it is the wrong thing to say at the wrong time.

Taking full notice of my mother's glare I decide it's best to change the subject.

"You know, Mom, every time I sit on one of these chairs I wonder what she used to think when she 'porch-sat.'"

My mom's face begins to soften.

"I'd say a lot of the same things you do. She worried about her children, same as you worry about Jonah. She used to get so scared if something happened to us that she couldn't fix. Sort of like you."

My mom settles comfortably into her seat, while I turn toward her to listen to the story I know will be forthcoming.

"One time, when your Uncle Jack was a little boy, he got into a nest of wasps. He got sicker and sicker as the day went on; and by nighttime, his face was swollen and purple. Mommy kept bathing the stings with a baking soda paste and sat up with him all night long. I remember waking up in the middle of the night and hearing Jack whimper. Mommy was praying. She prayed all through the night, with her Bible on her lap, asking God to take away her child's pain. She believed, and the next day the swelling began to go down. Just a couple of days later Jack was outside playing again."

"I can't imagine how scary that was for her. I would have called the doctor."

I shiver just thinking about what I would do if something like that happened to Jonah.

"But, you see, Cady, she didn't have that option sixty years ago. The doctor wasn't called, or even available to be called, every time something like that happened. It probably never occurred to her to call the doctor, so she called on the one she knew."

The corners of my mom's mouth turn up as she delivers her next line.

"It might do you some good, Cady, the next time you're feeling like the world has handed you a raw deal. Take a page from your grandmother's remedy book. It's laying in there on the coffee table."

I have to chuckle. She gets the last word . . . once again.

* * * * *

The next morning I grab the newspaper as soon as it hits the porch. The Sunday paper's classified ads have been significant in my quest for full-time employment over the past few months. My job search has not gone well up to this point, and I am more than a little discouraged. It seems that just a couple of years on the "mommy track," rather than the "fast track," has derailed my career, or so it seems to me. Usually I see little that interests me; but with the months rolling, the need to return to work occupies my thoughts most of the time. This particular Sunday a small ad catches my eye. Now, if my résumé can catch the employer's eye, my jobless state may be ready to change.

* * * * *

A few nights later, I slip out the back door as everyone else lay sleeping. It has been an incredibly joyous, but exhausting day. When the phone rang this morning, I answered, not knowing how much the call would change my life. Apparently, I was right about my luck changing. It turns out that the ad was for a small company which needed a Public Relations Director. The owners were impressed with my background and loved the

13

samples of work I sent to them. They called me immediately and wasted no time offering me a job. Who would have believed it a week ago?

So, here I sit by the zinnia bed tonight, a fully employed woman, now able to support myself and my child. One more piece of the puzzle of life is in place again . . . for the time being.

A year ago no one could have convinced me that I could handle so many changes . . . or that I could grow so much and become so strong. I thought I was strong, until one day when everything in the life and the reality I had known for eight years turned out to be false. I have tried so hard to put into words for people this past year, what that feels like.

Imagine that your house is burning down, what would you grab? Imagine your life crumbling down around you, what would you hold onto? I finally learned how to hold onto myself. I think God can do anything, but ultimately I had to make a choice.

Were the dreams I had of an intact family for my child, worth staying in a place I no longer felt safe? No, they weren't. Can you really live a full life with a man you no longer trust? No, you can't. Can you sleep well at night with a man who would gamble with your finances, risk your health, and ultimately your life, to pursue his own foolish pleasures? I know I couldn't. When I realized he didn't want to make any changes, I knew I had to be the one who did.

And today my life and my child's life are so much better. I planted a seed of faith the day I left my old life, and after a year of growing, it's time to reap. So I sit here, by the zinnia bed, in the still, cool springtime night, waiting for the flowers to bloom . . . and this time, I'll be here to see them.

Pam Keaton

Road Trip to Albany

Miles of board fencing and loose-laid creek rock walls line the country roads from Maysville to Lexington and on to Albany. I chose to take these roads on my first road trip in years without my husband at the wheel. When time is more of the essence, I am perfectly capable of joining the masses on the Interstate in hot pursuit of weekend life, liberty, and happiness. But for a peaceful weekend away with my mother and my niece, a long slow drive over maple tree-shaded state roads, no busier than those in my own county, seemed the better choice.

It was on this scenic excursion to a family reunion last year that I made three surprising discoveries. The first was how beautiful the green rolling hills of Appalachia are, peppered with grazing livestock and—well okay—salted with the welcoming white-pillar porches of historic farmhouses. The second was that although southern Ohio had been my home since my birth a few decades ago, there is no doubt that the warmly embrac'n, bright smil'n, guitar play'n, gospel sing'n inhabitants of Clinton County, Kentucky, are my people.

What was the third discovery? The most surprising—and distressing—discovery of all was that either the World had never actually revolved around me or, if it had, those days were over.

* * * * *

I hadn't really wanted to come on this trip in the first place. My mother's childlike understanding and personality as well as the possible medical reasons for it cannot be easily described in a few paragraphs. I'll just say that she always seems to be stumbling through life pointing and saying "I want that," with either no understanding of or no concern about consequences or payment plans. She is ever quick to assume that one of her four off-spring "safety nets" will be there to take care of things, and that is probably because one or more of us usually is there. At one time, each of us four girls has borne the responsibility of keeping Mom's household bills paid, taking her to the grocery store and doctor, and screening her mail—discreetly removing tempting catalogues.

My oldest sister, Gigi, took over those responsibilities a few years ago and has been—I am probably not as ashamed as I should be to say—taking care of Mom's physical needs the longest. Therefore, since I have not taken as much constant care of her day-to-day needs as I should, I tend to swoop in and help out in more social ways. I remind myself when she calls at the most inconvenient times not to chide her for calling to tell me for the third time something that I didn't care about the first time I heard it. I try to buy her gifts that she will like rather than simply something that she needs because her own money has to be spent in more responsible ways. I even take her out to dinner and a movie every now and then, although I have to be sure to choose a movie that will not have nudity, foul language, or much serious deep kissing unless I want to constantly be ssshhhing my mother who can't seem to experience shock, embarrassment, or incredulity in silence.

One of Mom's older sisters died a few years ago—a sister than she had only seen a handful of times since the rest of the family had moved to Ohio when Mom was eight years old. Since her sister's death, Mom has been talking on the telephone with the widower. The concept of men and how they are not all flirting with her is also a difficult one to get through to Mom. In her mind, any man who smiles or says friendly things is quite possibly interested in being her next husband, and her now-available former brother-in-law was no exception. Who knows? Maybe he has given her some reason to think that he is interested in her, but I tend to believe that he still thinks of her as a little sister. So it was perfectly natural for him to invite her to his family reunion in Albany—a road trip that Mom was absolutely determined to take.

Mother has never driven herself and so has depended upon the kindness of strangers, neighbors, and senior citizens organizations whenever family shuttles are not available. All of us girls tried to reason her out of this trip to a reunion for someone else's family, but she was not to be discouraged.

Once or twice a year Gigi and her family take a trip to Texas to visit my youngest sister. A few times, they have gone by car so that Mom—who is deathly afraid of flying—could go along; but they sometimes make the trip by airplane, leaving Mom behind. To soften the blow for her of feeling left out of these vacations, I usually take her to a nearby city and distract her with food, entertainment, and sometimes even an overnight stay. But when promising that type of compromise this time only resulted in her running through a list of elderly neighbors with cars, I decided to make the best of it. After all, I had promised to take her down to Albany at some time or another; and I do love traveling. Better still, my newly-graduated niece with as yet no full-time employment could come along and liven things up.

Misty is Gigi's daughter. Unfortunately I haven't been blessed with any children of my own so I have had my name put in the credits of Misty's life story and that of her slightly older brother, Jason. I lived with them during five of their most formative years when Gigi was newly divorced and I was not yet married. They all jokingly called me the "man of the house" because I was called upon for bug killing, minor tinkering, and driving on all long road trips. Although Gigi was and probably still is more intelligent than I am, the general consensus from the children at the time was that I was the "smart one around here." That was probably due for the most part to my spending many bedtime hours sharing what the kids called "true stories" as they bounced expectantly on my bed chanting those two words—much like the audience chants the rock star's name, urging the concert to begin. Hmmm.

The "true stories" were short remembrances of my childhood in which I learned some valuable moral or practical lesson while, of course, bruising either my body or my ego. I think that hearing my stories pleased the kids because it gave them actual evidence that adults have not always been big enough, tall enough, fast enough, smart enough, or pretty enough. I think it encouraged them and maybe even gave them a few life experiences to look forward to. During those five years, I hosted tea parties; swung them—squeaking with joy—in circles by their hands until we were all so dizzy we couldn't stand; made some of their Halloween costumes; and watched over them during the nights when their mother was working third shift. I read to them, let them sleep in bed with me, told them true stories, and went on vacations with them enough times that I think it may be safe to say that I secured the place as their favorite aunt. Don't ya think?

In their adolescent and earlier teenage years, since I was married by then, my role became more of periodic advisor for them both, and an occasional "girl's-night-out buddy" for Misty. It was definitely a change from when they had stood at the bottom of the stairs to my second floor rooms and politely inquired, "Aunt Lizzy? Can we come up?" as instructed by their mother.

My new role was as a more distant, and probably more typical, aunt figure, but was still comfortable. I did have a husband and less free time to spend with them, so I knew this to be the natural course of things.

Now, here, Mom, Misty, and I were on our first road-trip together with just the three of us. Misty and I would enjoy the scenery, music from the CD's we both had brought, the hotel amenities, and each other's witty banter. The strength of three, we knew, would make it bearable and maybe even fun carting Mom back to a town she had seen only a few times since the age of eight, but that she still thought of as home.

After breakfast in the small, Ohio River town of Aberdeen, we crossed the bridge into Maysville, Kentucky and were on our way. The gently rolling hills we passed were washed by a beautiful early morning fall sun. The road was newly paved with crisp yellow painted lines leading us on a peaceful ride past humble farmhouses, impressive horse estates, historic storefronts, and meticulously tailored golf courses all within just the first hour. Our listening pleasure had begun with a Johnny Mathis CD; which is one of my favorites. This "Heavenly" music was made years before my time; but hearing it always takes me to a time passed when people's behavior demonstrated a sense of class, even if their pocketbooks couldn't. The smooth rise and fall of the orchestra music and Johnny's soothing voice gliding through sappy love songs takes me to a paradise where people are carefree and blissfully in love. Who wouldn't love this music on a drive such as this?

The name Misty comes to mind. She listened politely but seemed unaffected by the music that pleased me so. Most of the songs were new to her so she could not join Johnny and me in the "oh you have got to hear this one" numbers that I played for her before deciding to give her a break.

Misty's idea of good traveling music on a day such as that was understandable at her age. It was a beautiful day; she felt good about herself; she was an independent woman just recently free of public education; and she was on a carefree tour of Eastern America. So, instead, we listened to Gretchen Wilson's CD and belted out the words to "Redneck Woman," "Here for the

Party," and "Homewrecker" while Mom sat in the back seat shaking her head and reminding me to keep my hands on the wheel and watch the road.

I am at an age where I can almost equally enjoy participating in goofy party games with kids, or playing scrabble and drinking coffee with senior citizens. I adore little children with their simple questions, happy dances, and excited faces as they make some new discovery; and I also respect and appreciate the wisdom and life experiences of the elderly. Now teenagers and young adults, I am finding, tend to disappoint me. I know it's only natural in that stage of life to be independent, cocky, and too excited about life and new experiences to remain devoted to all the gems you learned in Sunday school. I am disappointed, though, that with each passing generation, the memories seem to be shorter and shorter.

Misty's first decision as an adult was to get a tattoo just below the small of her back. Don't misunderstand. If I ever did believe that tattoo's were equal to "bad girl," my adoration of Misty tends to shake that assumption. It did say something to me, though, that she had felt the need to make some kind of bold announcement of her independence. It struck me as sort of like a person who reaches legal drinking age going out and getting smashed on the first night. I found it ironic that when a kid reaches the age where he or she is accredited with having the maturity to make decisions, they celebrate that new right by flaunting it with juvenile decisions.

Since Misty, however, was enrolled in nursing school; still attended church regularly and sang in the choir; still was, by far, more respectful and caring about her parents and other elders than most teenagers; and, as far as I know, had never drunk alcohol and was still a virgin, I decided to cut her some slack. Here again, it's not that I believe that listing to Gretchen Wilson songs equals "bad girl." But the Christian adult in me who took the time to listen to the words glorifying drinking, partying, and wearing tight pants to "watch the little boys come undone" did worry a bit about these ditties being Misty's choice of emotional outlet.

The second indicator that Misty was not my "little monkey girl" anymore was when we got to the hotel that evening. Gigi had given Misty the money she had been putting away for Mom's benefit, and Misty had put it in her very own checking account for which she had a shiny new Visa check card. Since the trip was Mom's idea, her money would be used for the hotel and expenses until it ran out. I knew that I would not be paying; but I had always been the information-getter, the decision-maker, the all-powerful overseer, if you will. So it was second nature for me to follow Misty into the hotel to make sure the check-in went smoothly.

"Aunt Liz?" Misty asked casually as we were walking back to the car. "Did you think that I didn't know how to pay for the room?" This loaded question was different from the "how" and "why" questions I was used to from her; so I let my brain crunch on it a bit, and realized what she was implying, and that she was right. There had been no real reason for me at the check-in counter. I had saved us $10 with my Triple A card, but I was getting the distinct impression that Misty would have gladly paid the $10 to have maintained the image of being "large and in charge" in front of the young male check-in clerk.

Wow! My young niece didn't need me to stand in front of her anymore and protect her from dogs. Truth be told, now she would most likely step in front of me and strangle an attacking canine with her bare hands. In the past few years, living with her dad, Misty has driven four-wheelers through mud holes, gone hunting with the men-folk, and doctored more animals with disgusting infections than I probably care to know about. I was beginning to get the picture that she could carry all the bags, lead Mom by the arm, and unlock the hotel door with her teeth, all without my supervision.

Later that night, I did manage not to comment on the extra skin that her new swimming outfit showed. I had no desire for the mood to become uncomfortable and had realized that my comments were not likely to produce desirable results anyway. Besides, since this was a small town hotel with very few guests, we had the pool room all to ourselves. Mom had stayed in the room to rest while Misty and I raced the length of the pool, competed for breath-holding stamina, and performed mock water ballet to our own operatic singing voices echoing off the walls. I did say that we had the room to ourselves, didn't I?

"I think I'll get up early and come down for a morning swim," Misty said.

"How early?" I asked.

"Oh, I don't know. Maybe about six."

I was hearing warning bells. My mother sleeps very lightly and for only a few hours at a time. She also worries to an unreasonable degree about things that would only be mildly stressful to most other people. If she sees a headline on a check-out stand tabloid about the World ending the following weekend, she calls everyone she knows to get reassurances from them that it's not true. While she would have some doubts about the rumors of space aliens taking over Texas, she would still worry for days and call to warn my little sister just in case.

I had heard that on one of the Texas trips that Gigi and her family took Mom on, Misty and Jason—both already teenagers by that time—had been entrusted by their mother to swim alone and come back to the room when finished. Gigi had not left my mother in any supervisory position while she and her second husband went for a walk, but Mom believed herself to be in charge. She wanted to go to the room herself, but was afraid to leave her teenage grandkids unattended for fear they might drown or get kidnapped. Misty and Jason are usually pretty good at dealing with their grandmother's hang-ups, but they felt justified in refusing to cut their swim short just to calm her unreasonable fears.

I was told that Mom threw a royal fit and made a scene before disappearing herself for a while, which was uncharacteristic of her. The scenes were characteristic. It was the disappearing that was not. Her sweet revenge by hiding in the hotel room closet, while everyone, including hotel workers, searched for her, succeeded in worrying and inconveniencing Gigi and her family. It also succeeded in them seriously considering not taking her on any more trips.

"Misty, you know your grandmother is going to throw a fit if you try to leave the room by yourself that early in the morning," I reminded her because she had obviously forgotten that earlier incident.

"Yeah. But I am eighteen."

Okay, this does kind of bug me. I know that at age eighteen, a child is free from the legal restraints of parents and basically every other adult in the world. But when I was eighteen, my dad had to remind me that it was not at all up to him anymore whether I took a trip to New York City on the money I had saved from my new job. Yeah, I knew it was not up to him anymore, but I still wanted to know that I would not be disappointing him if I went. If it had still been up to him, would he have let me go? Okay, his answer was "no" and I still went, but still. My point is that I was not adamant that midnight on day-one age eighteen was some magic portal into "nobody tells me what to do."

Of course it was LEGALLY up to Misty to decide when she would go swimming even if it worried her grandmother, and, subsequently, inconvenienced me. But it was not very thoughtful of her, and that was disappointing. I know some would say that I should not let the rantings of my mother run my life; and in truth, I usually don't. This was just one weekend. The rest of my life tends to be relatively unaffected by her worries and whims. Besides, I had argued and stamped my feet for the better part of the eighteen years that Mom was my legal authority. My mental health had actually gotten much better when I learned to remain calm and pick my fights. As I said, Misty and Jason were usually pretty good at handling Mom because they too had come to understand the value of using jokes or well-devised compromises instead of foot stamping. That was why it struck me as out of character for Misty to be so forceful about this.

"Well," I said. "If you want to swim, I'll come down here with you in the morning."

"Why?" Misty asked.

"Well, I know nothing would probably happen to you, but on the very off chance that something did . . . " I trailed off, thinking that would satisfy everyone. Misty would get her early morning swim, and Mom would not feel the need to make a scene as the guardian of the hotel room portal. But Misty didn't let it end there.

"Aunt, Liz. You do know that back home I go places by myself all the time, don't you? I go work out by myself, and I swim by myself all the time at the Y."

You would think that this would not have surprised me, but I had simply not stopped to think about it that way. It's true. She did spend all kinds of time by herself back home. This wasn't really all that different. I guess I had just been thinking that she was still my sister's little girl and I was responsible for her safety.

It turned out to be a non-issue, though, because after staying up late watching an in-room movie, Misty didn't care much for an early-morning swim. I had been relieved by that but not by her choice the night before to leave my proffered robe behind when she slipped, scantily clad, down to the car for my stash of microwave popcorn. Hey, it was a nice silk robe. It's not like I was asking her to wear floral flannel buttoned up to her chin. Don't worry. I get it. She's eighteen. She's eighteen. I kept my comments to myself.

My mother was the first one awake the next morning, showered, and anxiously trying to decide what to wear, laying the outfits out on the bed like a teenager getting ready for a date.

Misty and I both noticed this and found it to be touching, so we sprang into action. Misty hefted a large make-up kit from her travel bag, and for the next half hour, I dried and curled Mom's hair while Misty tastefully painted her face with various powders and liquids. "If you're gonna do it," we told her, "then let's do it right."

* * * * *

There was some time to kill before the reunion began, so we visited the cemetery where my grandparents and several other relatives are buried. Then we stopped in at the public library and found a comfortable wing-back chair for my mother while Misty and I spent some time in the local history room. Whether it was various church directories with black and white photos showing posing choir members and Sunday School classes, old transcribed marriage license records going back several decades, or local families immortalized in photographs of them posing in front of their homes, the names Honeycutt, Norris, Gross, and Shelley occurred again and again. I recognized those names as my grandmother's maiden name, my grandfather's family name, and the married names of two of my mother's older sisters.

I came across a photo of my grandmother's family, she being one of the younger of seven children who stood around their seated parents. It occurred to me that back in Ohio, there were no such photos or journal entries illustrating my family's roots. There couldn't be because both sides of my family had settled there from other places. I don't know exactly where my father's ancestors came from; but in the small town of Albany, Kentucky, recorded in the black and white of historic journals, roadside mailboxes, and decaying tombstones, I can see where I came from.

* * * * *

Misty and I had planned to drop Mom off at my ex-uncle's family reunion and carry in the lunchmeat and vegetable tray we had brought, but we had no intention of staying ourselves. Inside the church basement, we fully expected to find dozens of people who were baffled as to why three strangers from Ohio were intruding on their family time. Mom could stay there all day if she wanted to, but Misty and I would find something else to do.

From the time we stepped through the door and my mother was recognized as "Aunt Jane," we were all showered with smiles, introductions, and hugs. For the next half-hour while several ladies busily uncovered dishes and prepared for the meal, I uncovered my southern roots. I don't know why, but it had escaped me that even though my aunt had passed away, her children, grandchildren, and great-grandchildren were still my family. And there they were—smiling faces floating around us—as happy to see us, as if they had spent years waiting for us to come back down the road. I saw my beloved grandmother many times in the faces of the confident southern women who emerged to welcome me. If there had been any doubts left that I was thought of as an intruder, they faded completely when yet another set of my grandmother's eyes looked into mine and a steady southern female voice declared, "Well, Honey, I don't know who ya are, but I know ye're in the raaht place."

Having been to countless church dinners in Ohio, the concept of a large variety of hot food on one table is not unfamiliar to me. But I believe it's safe to say that this array of country cooked food which included fried chicken, stuffed peppers, mashed potatoes, various vegetable dishes, and a wide assortment of casseroles and desserts was the largest and most satisfying feast I have ever had the pleasure of partaking in. It should not surprise you that I hid the cold lunchmeat and raw vegetable tray in a nearby refrigerator, 'cause that was just embarrassing.

When I got my plate, I looked around to check on Mom and Misty, neither of whom I had seen since we got there. Mom was seated at a table surrounded by women older than me who knew her only from photographs and from a few short visits to Ohio, but who kept addressing her as "Aunt Jane" as naturally as Misty and Jason talking to me. Mom was telling them about her "girls" and their families, about her life at the "Commons" (which are government-subsidized apartments newly built in our hometown) and about her mental health support group meetings. Her audience took it in and traded her with updates about their lives. Contrary to the chilly reception I had expected my mother to get here, she was completely accepted simply for being "Aunt Jane" and was having the time of her life. At that moment, I felt a complete love for my mother. No matter how unskilled my sisters and I had always found her to be at teaching, listening, or other things commonly regarded as real parenting, she had never been short on hugs and kisses; and she would have tackled a bear if it had been trying to hurt us. We had all stumbled our way through our lives together, but we had all turned out all right.

Misty was three rows away from me at a table filled with faces that could not be familiar to her; but she, too, was having a blast. She was leaning over toward an elderly lady at her right who must have been confusing her for one of my sisters because she was telling Misty that she was an old friend of our grandmother, Georgia. Misty, who had picked up on the woman's inferior hearing, was sweetly and loudly correcting her but urging her not to worry about it and to go on with her story. At the table across from Misty were the twelve-year-old twin granddaughters of one of my cousins. They had anxiously come to meet me when they had seen their grandmother introducing herself. The girls had been happy to make my acquaintance, but they were obviously entranced by Misty. Misty had greeted the girls with warm hugs and had set off immediately becoming their adored 5'9", blonde, beautiful, eighteen-year-old idol. All pug noses, freckles, blonde locks, and braces, they had been by her side since that first meeting listening to her and answering her questions about their hobbies and their lives. Misty had not needed to stay by my side as she might have in earlier years. On the contrary, she had stepped confidently into her own role as nurturer and entertainer.

After dinner someone said the word "guitar," and I heard a chorus of chair legs scraping the floor as a clearing was made at the front of the room. It had been a long time since I had experienced a country song fest. Before my grandmother passed away when I was eighteen, her children had often hosted birthday parties for her at local parks. Since singing and guitar picking had been the main pastime for the settlers from Kentucky, two or three did not gather together without a guitar being within arm's reach. We never went home from a birthday party, family reunion, or Sunday visit without several hours of playing and singing.

My sisters and I never knew how to play the guitar, but we soon stood out for our singing. We were often urged up on stage to sing something we knew—most often from our church songbooks. It didn't matter that my uncles and their buddies didn't have the music because all we girls had to do was start singing; and one by one, as they picked up the beat and the key, our accompanists would join in at full volume. After my grandmother died, the song fests were fewer and much farther between until they were almost just a memory. Now here I was hearing the same style of strumming and the same crooning southern voices even though none of the faces was the same. Well, not exactly the same.

It wasn't long before my mother, true to form, started spreading the word that her girls were good singers. There was only Misty and me, but she—as well as her brother—had become quite a singer, and I was still pretty good at it myself. The occasion never arose, however, that the audience would be enthralled by our amazing northern voices. I wasn't sure they were even hearing mine. I was used to singing lead when I sang with my sisters because they were so much better at picking out the alto, tenor, and bass notes; and my voice was clearer and smoother for the lead. But now, I was singing with Misty, who was also used to singing lead. And we were both competing with one of my older female cousins who was swinging her fist and stomping her foot while she belted out the songs louder than either of us.

My annoyance at having to compete with two other voices brought with it a realization about myself. This cousin of mine, who was possibly 15 years my senior, still had a pretty face and sparkling eyes; and, throughout the day so far had stood out in my mind as the spunkiest of her sisters or her female cousins. She reminded me of an older, southern version of myself, obviously accustomed to commanding attention from young people as well as adults and taking a backseat to no one. Misty, on my other side, has a voice that will crack or veer off key if she is not well practiced; but when steadied by confidence or harmonizing voices, hers is as beautiful and clear as any professional country singer I have ever heard. Why shouldn't she be singing the lead?

Could it be that my reluctance to comprehend and accept that Misty was now a capable adult was more than disappointment that her choices and decisions were sometimes at odds with my own? Could it be that I could see myself one day sitting in the audience listening instead of being on stage? Or riding in the backseat on road trips while Misty and her niece—or maybe the adoring twins—ride in the front laughing, singing along with Gretchen Wilson, and rolling their eyes when I shake my head and remind Misty to keep her hands on the wheel and watch the road?

* * * * *

Mom did not leave the reunion with her former brother-in-law as a boyfriend, but I suspect that she hadn't had any serious expectations along those lines. She had likely been more like a girl going to a school dance to see who might be there and what might happen. Misty left with two twelve-year-old girls hugging her neck and hanging on her as she promised them she would be back next year whether her grandma and Aunt Lizzy came or not.

I left with telephone numbers and an assignment to create the family tree because, as my mother loudly announced when they were looking for volunteers, "Liz is real good on the computer!" I had tried to decline, saying that I thought it should be someone who was more familiar with all of their names. I had wanted to flatly refuse because I didn't want the responsibility, but they insisted they would help me with the particulars. I did have an entire year for the appropriate inspiration to strike, so I gave in.

As I drove north through the town that final time, I pictured my family tree as a blossoming magnolia deeply rooted in the rust-colored southern soil—some of its flowers missing due to their migration to parts unknown. As I remembered the smiling faces we had just left, a vision of my grandmother came to mind. She was sitting in her front porch lounge chair smiling with her arm raised high over her head and her hand flapping an exaggerated good-bye. "I'll see ya agin, but I caint say when!" she used to call.

My grandmother, who I had so adored for her warm hugs, hearty belly laughs, and blackberry dumplings, had been a granddaughter, daughter, sister, wife, mother, grandmother, and long-time friend to people in this town long before I came to know her in Ohio.

As I watched the familiar names on mailboxes sail past one last time, I had an incredible feeling of belonging. I had no intention of packing up and moving down here, but I had the warmly comforting feeling of knowing that if I did, somewhere, farther back on the tree, a blossom would form so similar in size, color, and fragrance that no one would know or care that it hadn't been there all along.

* * * * *

The weather and the passing scenery were as beautiful as they had been on the trip down, but we were all a bit more subdued, the excitement being over. Misty and I discussed our new acquaintances while Mom dozed in the back seat. We listened in silence for quite a while to Misty's CDs and then made one last stop for dinner before crossing the bridge back into Ohio. Here I received the last evidence that Misty's future life would never again be dependent upon my input or opinions.

It happened that the waiter for our table was a very courteous and not unattractive straight-laced kind of young man. He returned to our table often and smiled sweetly, his eyes drifting shyly to Misty every time. Mom and I both softly teased Misty about the attention she was getting, but she was more interested in the attention she was getting from the two rougher-looking young men seated at the table behind us. They were both more casually dressed in jeans and boots, and at least one of them had a closely shaved head, a beard, and tattoos peeking out from underneath his T-shirt sleeves. I only saw this one as we left the restaurant because he had been facing us. He didn't appear to notice me and either didn't know or didn't care that I could hear him as he read to his buddy the lettering on Misty's T-shirt. The logo that ran across her chest was nothing provocative and certainly nothing that a disinterested casual passerby would take an interest in. But then, it was obvious by his smiling eyes that the man wasn't exactly disinterested.

As it happened, neither was Misty. She didn't stop to speak to the men, but she had given them a grin and was obviously more uplifted by the attention from them than she had been by the attention from the waiter. I had hoped that the rough-n-tough music that she preferred to bounce to had been mostly because of its fast-paced beat and her youthful exuberance and not that it had any deeper roots in her morals, opinions, or life choices.

31

"Misty," I began after a few silent miles. "I know that not every guy who dresses and looks like those guys back there is a bad guy. But I hope you remember that they're not all your dad or your brothers."

Misty has a couple of stepbrothers from her dad's second marriage. I don't know them, but from her stories I surmise that they probably don't dress and behave like choirboys; but there can be no doubt that they have also earned Misty's enduring love and trust. Apparently while I was telling her stories and hosting pretend tea parties on weekdays, her brothers were showering her with rough-n-tough brotherly love on the weekends at her Dad's house.

My opening sentence began what I knew was probably my last unsolicited outpouring to Misty of my observations and experiences from when I was a young woman stepping into the world on my own. I didn't yell or degrade her in any way. I merely expressed disappointment in an entire generation of young people—not just her—who seemed to be more interested in having a good time doing whatever they want to do than in thinking more deeply about the important things in life and the characteristics of a solid marriage and home. Specifics are not important here. What is important is that when I was finished, Misty wasn't sad or angry. She wasn't enlightened or transformed either—not that I really expected to have rocked her world. What her eyes held instead was a pleasant expression of calm assurance as she responded with a smile.

"Aunt Lizzy. You think way too much."

* * * * *

We rode in silence for a several minutes until we noticed that Mom had begun softly singing to herself as she rested her head against the window. "Amazing Grace, how sweet the sound that saved a wretch like me." Misty and I began to sing too, me taking the lead and she doing a beautiful job of harmonizing. We continued throughout the verses singing slowly and softly to the beloved words not realizing that Mom had dropped off to listen. When we got to the end of the verses, I began a final verse that I have heard done in a couple of churches I have visited. The entire verse is sung with two words over and over again. "Praise God. Praise God. Praise God. Praise God. Praise God. Praise God. Praise God. Praise God. Praise God. Praise God. Praise God. Praise God. Praise God. Praise God."

We slowed the final praises—placing meaningful emphasis on the words—with me raising and lowering my voice through several added notes and Misty masterfully harmonizing along to a truly beautiful end.

We were both letting our minds absorb the meaningful words in a satisfied silence when suddenly there was a shriek from the back seat that made both Misty and me scream in fear. I jerked the wheel, certain that my mother had seen something in the road that I was bound to hit. Then as Mom's entire sentence registered in our minds, we laughed so hard at ourselves that our stomachs ached. "Aaaat was beautiful!" Mom had declared about our performance.

Her outburst had been so unexpected and was so forceful that the first word, pronounced the way she had pronounced it, had sounded like a fearful shriek of warning. Whenever we tell the story about our road trip to Albany, this rush of adrenaline is what we remember and laugh about the most.

* * * * *

Having a husband and other responsibilities, I cannot commit myself to trips away from him very far in advance; so when my mother began one week after our return asking if I was going to take her again this year, I could only tell her "We'll see."

Misty, however, assures her grandmother that she'll take her even if I can't. My mother is not as confident as I am that Misty is perfectly capable of getting them safely back to Albany; so she will sit in her apartment and worry about it all year until we see if I can take the time off again.

Misty has begun nursing school along with a full-time job. She gets very little sleep, and I only see her for a few minutes after church services and for a few hours every month or so when I go to her mother's for Sunday dinner. She still greets me with a warm hug and "Aunt Lizzy!" the way she has done ever since I can remember, but I have come to accept now that I have become like my Aunt Beulah—my mom's smart, strong, hard working, talented, funny, and very opinionated older sister— who I remember fondly, but who doesn't have any real impact on my day-to-day life.

I know Misty will be sad if she reads this because she has a soft heart and doesn't like the idea of growing apart from her loved ones. But I will tell her the same thing I have told myself—that this is the natural course of life. Sure, I wish that when she was a child, and I was helping to instill confidence and strength within her, that I had remembered to insert a magical place mark in her brain to always hover around Aunt Lizzy and do everything that Aunt Lizzy thinks is right. But, oh well.

I'll just live my own life—loving my husband, writing my stories, painting my pictures—and learn to settle into this new phase of being Good Old Aunt Liz.

Or I could talk my husband into moving to Texas. My little sister has two young daughters, and there's another one on the way; so I hear there is a growing demand for "True Stories" down there.

Jennifer Mullins

Cooking for the Dead

By the time he had finished the walk home from his night shift job, Aaron Hart knew that someone in the neighborhood had died. His wife Annie met him at the door to confirm the news.

"Miss Chloe died last night," she told him.

"I know," he said.

"But how could you?" Annie asked. "It just happened a few hours ago."

"Kitchen lights on all through the neighborhood. I've smelled everything from chicken fryin' to chocolate cake bakin', and I'm starved. Feed me now, woman," he said, giving his wife a slap on the backside.

It occurred to Annie that she should chide her husband for his irreverent behavior in the face of death, but she didn't have the heart to do it. As always, she felt such relief that he had made it home in one whole piece that she could only kiss him and feed him and tuck him into bed.

She, like the rest of the women in the neighborhood, was also honoring the southern tradition of cooking food to take to the home of the recently departed. Like at least one of her neighbors, if her husband's sense of smell was accurate, she was frying chicken. She had also baked biscuits that had, to her delight, turned out splendidly This seemed a proper tribute to Miss Chloe, since it was she who had taught Annie how to make biscuits.

Annie was married for all of eight months when she had begun to feel like she was the worst wife in the world. Everything she did seemed to be wrong. She couldn't make the collars stand up on Aaron's dress shirts when she ironed them. She couldn't get her biscuits to rise. Worst of all she couldn't even get pregnant. If her mother wasn't nagging her about when they were going to have a baby, his mother was.

One day when she could stand it no longer, she went to see her neighbor Chloe Miller and told her the whole miserable story. "Why, Annie, you're a fine little wife." Miss Chloe had told her. "And as for having a baby, that'll happen in time. It almost always does. You just take my advice and relax. Enjoy that man of yours while it's just the two of you." Chloe paused here for a moment and moved closer to Annie as if she were about to tell her a secret. "Honey, my grandmother used to say that God chose to bless women in a peculiar fashion. I think you'll find that what she said was true. Children are a most peculiar blessing."

Miss Chloe had laughed when Annie told her how she had been making biscuits and said it was no wonder they didn't rise. Then she had taught her how to make biscuits that rose up into perfect golden mounds every time. And she had been right. Four months later, Annie was pregnant with Aaron, Jr. Then just six months after Aaron, Jr. was born, she found herself pregnant again; this time with double blessings, Rachel and Leah.

Annie Hart cried a little while she stacked the warm biscuits in a basket. "I'll miss having you to talk to, Miss Chloe," she said. Then, feeling suddenly hungry, she took one of the biscuits from the basket and sat down at her kitchen table to enjoy it in the rare stillness before her three "peculiar blessings" awoke to eat up the rest of her day.

Directly across the street from the Hart house, Martha Campbell ladled meringue on top of her special key lime pie. She had learned how to make it when she and her husband had visited their son in Atlanta, and she thought it to be an elegant alternative to the plain country fare most of the neighborhood ladies cooked.

Martha sighed when she thought of Chloe, although she didn't feel particularly sad. Chloe had been dying for years. She had had rheumatic fever as a child and her heart was weak. Martha, now, was as healthy and hearty as a teen-ager. She had no reason to worry.

She was well-fixed, too, as her Mama used to say. Joe Campbell, her husband, was a pharmacist, and he made good money, a lot more than most of the men in town who worked in the coal mines that Martha hated so. It didn't matter how many times Dr. Campbell reminded her that it was the mines that kept his drugstore in business, Martha still felt as if she had risen above the scruffy little hole in the Appalachian mountains where she was forced to live. If only Dr. Campbell would agree to move to Atlanta where their son lived, Martha would be in a place where her refined manners and good taste would be appreciated.

As it were, she took some small measures to make the best of her situation. She insisted that everyone call her husband Dr. Campbell, and that they as a couple be referred to as Dr. and Mrs. Campbell. She even signed the invitations to her Christmas party that way, "Dr. and Mrs. Campbell request the pleasure of your company at their annual Christmas soiree." Most of the people who were invited didn't even know what a soiree was, and they all howled with laughter at the yearly invitations. It was generally said in town that Martha Campbell always had to "cut the biggest hog in the ass."

Martha slid her pie into the oven of the only electric stove in town, and sat down at her kitchen table to have a cup of tea while the meringue browned. She tried to have pleasant thoughts about Chloe. She was, after all, a good Christian woman, but she couldn't help that she didn't like her.

It had started when they were still young girls, and Martha had fallen head over heels in love with Joe Campbell. They were at the annual Church picnic and she had followed him and his friend Bill when they had slipped away to hide behind a thicket of trees to chew tobacco. She eavesdropped, hoping that she might hear something that would confirm that Joe was as crazy about her as she was about him.

"Hey, who you reckon would win if we had one of them beauty contests at the county fair?" she heard Bill ask.

"Wouldn't be no contest," Joe had answered, and Martha's heart had begun to beat faster. "Everybody knows Chloe Smith is the prettiest girl in town."

Now, after they were married, Joe had sworn he didn't really mean it. But it still rankled in Martha's heart, and she did not like Chloe. There was something else that troubled her, too. Sometimes she could almost swear that Chloe felt sorry for her, although she knew this was just a foolish notion. Why would Chloe pity her when it was she who had a well-to-do husband and lived in the nicest house on the block?

Martha took her pie from the oven, and her face fell when she looked at it. The color was all wrong, too dark a green, not light and refreshing as it should look, and the meringue had cracked and fallen. It made her feel unbearably sad to look at it, and frightened in a way she hadn't felt in years. She wanted to run to the closest mirror and check to be sure her own face wasn't as cracked and fallen as the dilapidated meringue on her special key lime pie.

She sat back down at the kitchen table and wondered where Chloe was right this minute. Perhaps her spirit was still here. She might even be in Martha's kitchen, watching her and reading her thoughts, feeling sorry for her like she had when she was still living. She told herself she was just being foolish, but she did feel almost as if Chloe were right in the chair beside her.

"Go away, Chloe," she said to the empty kitchen chair. "I don't need your pity."

Maggie Taylor could see into Martha Campbell's kitchen from her bedroom window next door. The fancy white Priscilla curtains blocked most of her view, but she caught occasional flashes of Martha's red apron as she moved about her kitchen. "Lord have mercy on us all," she thought. "She's probably making that sour ole' green pie again."

She turned from the window and went into the kitchen to take a peep at her own pie which was browning in the cook stove's oven. The smell of apples and spices filled the little kitchen and made the morning seem almost festive, as if it were a holiday, a time of celebration instead of a time of mourning. Maggie supposed that one could call death a celebration of sorts. That is, of course, if one believed that the dead might move on to collect some fine Heavenly reward. Sinner that she was, she wasn't so sure that she wanted to believe in the divine system of rewards and punishments in the afterlife.

She thought about all the meals she had cooked in this kitchen—piles of fried chicken, mountains of potatoes, corn bread fritters to reach the moon. She was tired of cooking, and at one time, she had loved it so. But, it was cooking that had started her on the path to sin.

She had felt so sorry for Chloe's husband Martin. Chloe's health had begun to fail before she was out of her thirties. Their only child had already married and left home, and poor Martin seemed at loose ends most of the time. Once, when Chloe was in the hospital, Maggie had gone to the house and informed him that she was going to cook him a decent breakfast before he went to work. All the neighborhood ladies had been making dinners and carrying them to him, but it had seemed to Maggie that Martin was as much in need of company as he was of food.

He had seemed delighted to have someone to talk to that morning. "You know," he had told her, "I think what I miss the most when Chloe's not here is having someone in the kitchen with me in the morning for breakfast. It's always the hardest part of the day."

She hadn't meant to kiss him, but he just seemed so lonely and sad and in need of a human touch. He had responded to her with such eagerness that she quickly realized that Chloe's company at breakfast wasn't the only thing he had been missing. They were both sorry afterwards, or at least they told each other they were, and they swore it would never happen again; and it didn't—not until the next time Chloe went into the hospital. Over the years, it became a pattern, an expectation, part of his life and part of hers.

She had felt terrible guilt, of course. All the preacher had to do was mention adultery in his Sunday sermon, and she could almost feel the flames of hell licking at her feet. She came to terms with guilt, though; and, until the day he died, Martin was as much her man as he was Chloe's.

She wondered if Chloe would haunt her now, or if she might come, like a succubus in the night, to take her own live husband in exchange for Martin.

Maggie took her apple pie from the oven and found it to be perfect. She placed it on the windowsill to cool, and went to sit in a kitchen chair and think about Chloe; but she couldn't. All she could think about was how good that pie smelled and how badly she wanted to cut herself a piece of it. She told herself that she couldn't possibly, and then she laughed out loud. "I might as well," she thought. "Forgive me, Chloe," she said aloud, as she cut into the still warm pie.

The sound of Maggie Taylor's kitchen window closing after she had removed her cooling apple pie from the windowsill traveled easily through the still morning air. Next door, Amanda Johnson wondered what kind of pie it was. She opened her own kitchen window which was only a few feet across from Maggie's and took a quick sniff of the air. "Apple," she said out

loud to no one in particular since she was alone, "Very appropriate for a temptress, Maggie." She closed her window and began
the process of cleaning up her kitchen before she left to take the
rice pudding she had just removed from the oven to Chloe's
house. Rice pudding was Chloe's favorite dessert. It was one of
the few foods she would eat in the last few weeks of her life, and
Amanda had delighted in making it for her. She didn't care if
any of the other mourners liked it or not. Her pappy had called
this particular ritual "cooking for the dead," and perhaps he had
been right after all. It was Chloe she was cooking for, not her
mourners. They could throw it in the trash if they didn't want it.

Amanda was angry. She made a great deal of noise as she
worked, throwing pots into the sink, banging dishes together
and mumbling to herself. "Harlot," she said, looking out her
window and into Maggie's kitchen. She couldn't see her, but she
knew she was still in there, biding her time until she could find
some other woman's husband to steal. She wanted to call Maggie a whore; but she couldn't make herself say the word out loud,
even alone in her own kitchen. She hated being so prim, but she
had been raised to be a lady. Her mother would be shocked at
her for even having such unChristian thoughts about another
human being, but her mother never had to carry the burden of
sordid secrets that Amanda shouldered.

She knew that good friends should be able to share their
burdens, but sometimes she wished that Chloe had just kept her
painful secrets locked inside like most women did. To her credit,
she did keep them to herself for most of her life; but toward the
end she appeared to weaken emotionally as well as physically;
and it seemed that she could no longer keep quiet about things
that were better left unspoken.

"Sometimes I wish I'd never had a child," she had said to
Amanda one morning when they were having their morning
coffee together.

"Chloe, you know you don't mean that," Amanda had said.

"Yes, I do. The Lord only knows how much I love my boy, but I lost my last few ounces of strength giving birth to him and raising him. There just weren't nothin' left for me to give Martin. Maybe if I hadn't had a child, I could have kept my man."

"Why, what are you talking about, Chloe? Martin Miller would have crawled through hell fire for you."

That was when Chloe had told her about Martin and Maggie Taylor. He had confessed everything to her himself a few weeks before he died.

Amanda wasn't sure who she hated the most after that, Maggie or Martin. She thought Martin to be the worst kind of traitor and a coward to boot. Why had he had to assuage his own conscience before he died by confessing his miserable indiscretions to Chloe? And perhaps she even began to hate Chloe a little after that day. Not just for burdening her with such knowledge, but also for her obstinate refusal to blame either her philandering husband or her harlot of a neighbor.

"Martin was still young when I got so sick," Chloe had told her. "He needed physical love, and I couldn't give him that anymore. He never stopped loving me and he took care of me with the patience of Job. I can't hate him for taking some pleasure for himself the last few years of his life, and I can't hate Maggie for giving him what I couldn't." Chloe and Amanda had been friends since they were sixteen, and this was the first serious conversation concerning sex they had ever had. Amanda knew they would not have had it then if it weren't for the fact that Chloe had been desperate for a confidant.

It was Chloe's nature to love and to forgive people, just as it was Amanda's nature to carry a grudge to the grave. Chloe couldn't dislike anybody, not even snooty ole' Martha Campbell.

"I feel right sorry her," she told Amanda, when everyone else in town was laughing over her silly Christmas soiree. "She doesn't want to be who she is, and it's like she's all the time scared people will realize that she's still just little ole' Martha

Jewell in her sister's hand-me-downs. It must be a terrible way to live."

That was Chloe, always practicing the virtues that everyone else just talked about.

"Well, what did it get you in the end, Chloe?" Amanda asked the empty air, "A sick bed for the last years of your life and a cheating husband. If that's what being a saint yields, then I guess I'll just stay a sinner."

Amanda was dabbing at tear-stained eyes when she started down her walkway on the way to Chloe's house. She was dismayed to hear Maggie's door open. She had hoped to avoid her. "Whore," she mumbled under her breath. There, she had said it, and she did feel better, even if no one had heard her.

"I'm sorry, Mrs. Johnson, did you say something," Annie Hart asked as she caught up to her neighbor. She was carrying a basket of what smelled like fried chicken and biscuits.

"No, dear, just talking to myself," Amanda said. "Come on and we'll go together."

"Yes, let's do," Annie said. "Here comes Mrs. Taylor, and there's Martha Campbell on her porch. We can all go together. Miss Chloe would like that."

Lisa Hall

Enjoy!

Lisa Hall

Party Line

Snoops, butt-in-skies, busy-bodies, yentas, meddlers, the women of Fletcher Hollow, Kentucky are none of these. We are just concerned, concerned about the welfare, strife, and joys of our neighbors. Thank goodness technology has aided us in our mission to tap into the needs of those around us. Yes, twenty-eight of the fifty or so households in the town are on party lines. Luckily, I am a member of one of these households.

It seemed like forever and a day before the phone company strung lines in Fletcher Hollow. That poor Alva Meyers has a son who was stationed in Fort Knox after he signed up for the Army. She'd get a ride to Pikeville every Sunday afternoon just so she could talk to him. You see, her sister married a coal operator's son from Pikeville. They built a stately brick house and lived high on the hog. That man turned out to be no good. He cheated on her, but not before leaving her with a house full of babies. She did get to keep the brick house. That house was one of the first within two hours of Fletcher Hollow to get a phone line. Velma talked to him every Sunday, until he was sent off to Germany to fight in the war. The saddest thing happened. He was taken as a prisoner of war about two weeks after he got over there. Some G.I.'s from his outfit rescued him two days later. That boy's been back for almost seven years now. He still doesn't seem right. Awful, the things they did to him! Alva is on that

45

same party line as me, so I've heard about some of the stuff they did. The atrocities of war are almost unspeakable!

I take Alva a pecan pie once a month. In fact, I take it on the second Tuesday of every month. You see, that's when her son visits, unless he has one of his scheduled mental health check ups at the VA Hospital in Johnson City. Then, he comes on Thursday. In that case, I take the pie over on Wednesday after church. Velma's son loves pecan pie. His wife doesn't cook, and Alva doesn't make good pecan pie. Trudy Blevins tasted it once and told me it was terrible!

Speaking of Trudy, her husband Carl has been ill for a good number of years. The men in his family never live very long. His daddy died at fifty, his brother at forty-six. Of course his daddy drank like a fish and his brother smoked two packs a day. You can hardly blame either one of them. His daddy had a really sad childhood; and his brother was married to the most atrocious, hateful woman. She was always nagging at him. He likely took up smoking just to have an excuse to get away from her. She'd never let him smoke in the house. She said smoke would stain their white living room sofa yellow. Anyhow, Carl has never been a partaker of cigarettes or whiskey; yet he seems to have fallen under the curse of his family.

His internals are full of stones; first gall, then kidney. The last gallstone attack came on about five years ago. Carl was working out in their yard. When Trudy went to the front door to summons him to dinner, she thought he was dying. He doubled over in pain, clammy, and white as a sheet. Trudy picked up to call for an ambulance and Lucille Smith was on the phone talking to her Aunt Betty. Usually it's like pulling teeth to get Lucille off the phone, but when Trudy explained that she had an emergency, Lucille not only got off the phone; she came down to their house to help Trudy pack her husband's bag for the hospital.

They did emergency surgery to remove his gall bladder. Carl nearly died when he came down with a staff infection during his recuperation. The funniest thing though, when he got out of the hospital, his doctor gave him a jar with his gall stones in it. Dr. Denton told Carl about a jeweler in Wise that makes pieces from polished gall stones. So he surprised Trudy with a lovely ring and matching pendant for their thirty-first anniversary. Not long after the gall stone attack, Carl began getting kidney stones. He no sooner passes one than he gets another one.

Back, to Alva's pecan pie. Alva needed to call her daughter Melissa when she picked up on Trudy. Trudy was on the phone, pouring her heart out to the pastor's wife. She was describing the excruciating pain Carl was suffering. Trudy was desperately trying to hold herself together for Carl. Between taking him to appointments and staying up with him at night when his attacks came on, she was exhausted. Alva wasn't trying to listen in, but she was in a hurry to call her daughter. Party line etiquette dictates that if you really need to make a call, you politely mention it to the party on the line who then is to end their call. Alva couldn't bear to make Trudy end her call. She was obviously in need of her pastor's wife's spiritual guidance. So, all poor Trudy could do was to sit and listen. Luckily, Trudy did have a box of stationary close to the phone. So, she was able to catch up on some of her correspondence while sitting there. Alva was on that phone for another forty-five minutes before she hung up. Alva felt so sorry for Trudy that she made her a nice dinner and took it to her house the next day. Everything was delicious, except for the pecan pie.

That's where I stepped in. Most people in Fletcher Hollow call me "Miss Pecan Pie" even though I'm a Mrs.; and my name is really Velma Cairns. Years ago, I entered a national contest sponsored by The Georgia Pecan Growers Association. I won second place among three-thousand applicants. My picture was in every newspaper in Eastern Kentucky. I won a free trip to Atlanta, and I get a case of pecans sent to me every three months for the rest of my life. Such accomplishments are never forgotten in a small town, and I am honored to be known for my pecan pie. With my ever-plentiful supply of pecans, I consider it my duty to make at least one pie a week. That pie that I make during the second week of every month has Alva's name on it! Now that I have explained my claim to fame, let me get back to Alva and Trudy.

Alva got so worried about Trudy that she forgot all about calling her daughter. Melissa was going to Morehead State University. She got a degree to be a school teacher, the first person in the family to even finish high school. Of course, Trudy and her husband Jimmy are just proud as peacocks.

Since Trudy forgot to call her daughter, Melissa called her the next morning. It seems Melissa had gotten serious with a boy at the college and wanted to bring him home to meet them. Trudy cleaned, polished, and cooked for a week. The day before Melissa and that boy were supposed to arrive Melissa called home in absolute distress. That boy broke up with her so that he could pursue some city strumpet from Roanoke!

Melissa was so distraught that Trudy and Jimmy drove over to Morehead to get her that night. Melissa barricaded herself in their house for about five days. Etta Cosby stopped by there to return a saw that her husband had borrowed from Jimmy. She said Melissa had red swollen eyes, like she'd been crying really hard. She'd also gained about fifteen or twenty pounds since her last visit home. Etta wondered if that boy broke up with her because she had gotten heavier. Melissa has a real pretty face and is smart as a whip, but some boys are shallow like that.

Speaking of Etta, that woman is the sweetest thing! She's got the tenderest heart in the state of Kentucky. Etta doesn't have much in the way of money, but she'd give her last dime to help someone else. She's always taking toys to orphans and knitting afghans for elderly people. Etta knows that trying to amass riches on earth is futile. Much greater riches await her in Heaven. There will be a special place up there for that precious soul and lots of jewels in her crown. The woman almost never says an unkind word about anybody. Her husband was the only person she told about Melissa's weight gain. He called her from work right after she'd returned from Trudy's house. Too bad, that nosy Barbara Dinsmore picked up on the conversation.

Barbara picks up while other people are talking on purpose. She doesn't care about her friends and neighbors. Barbara Dinsmore is just a gossip! To make things worse, her daughter Janine has always been jealous of Melissa. So, it just made Barbara's day when she heard Etta telling her husband that Melissa had gained weight.

Janine's resentment towards Melissa came to a head in third grade. Both girls were in the running for third grade princess at the school's Fall Carnival. Janine concocted a smear campaign, directed right at Melissa and her family. The most hurtful rumor was that she witnessed Melissa's daddy kissing their teacher on the lips. Melissa's daddy used to pick her up everyday after school. One day he showed up a little early to help Miss Novak move decorations for the carnival into the gymnasium. Janine claimed that she went to the gym to tell Ms. Novak that Elmer Hooven was getting sick and needed to go home. There she said she saw the two kissing. It's simply wasn't true! Now, Melissa's daddy is a nice looking man, but not the type to stray.

Janine's sinister scheme backfired. The other kids saw right through her false statements. None of the students voted for Janine. Melissa won by a landslide. All of the kids clapped and cheered as Melissa was crowned. Janine stood in the center of the gym floor with a scowl on her face. After the crowning Janine threatened to hit Melissa over the head with her Mary Jane. Principal Conners saw Janine taking off her shoe and sensed trouble. He quickly diverted Janine's attention by telling her that she needed to put her shoe back on because they weren't done taking pictures. The relationship between the two girls has been unpleasant ever since. If Principal Conners hadn't intervened in the Mary Jane incident, who knows? Melissa may have wound up with a concussion.

Janine couldn't wait to tell anyone who'd listen that Melissa had put on weight. She began her campaign at church, no less. It was a covered dish Sunday and Gigi Watkins came out of the line with a skimpy plate. When Gigi sat down in the fellowship hall, Fred Atwell noted rather loudly that Gigi must have not found much that she liked. A red-faced Gigi explained that she was trying to loose the rest of her baby weight. Fred Atwell tends to be quick on the draw with jokes and comebacks. There was a collective sigh of relief when he made no mention that Gigi's baby was seven years old. Gigi wound up sitting at the same table as Janine. Janine, of course, used the situation as an opportunity to discuss Melissa's weight. "Gigi, I wouldn't worry about a little baby weight. You oughta see Melissa. She looks like a stuffed sausage and she doesn't even have any kids."

Gigi, being a good Christian woman, quickly changed the subject. Unfortunately, a few people, including Etta, heard Janine's comment. Because they all knew about the history between Janine and Melissa, it was assumed that Janine was blowing smoke. After all, nobody had laid eyes on Melissa during her last visit home, except for Etta.

Etta prayed that chatter about Melissa's weight gain did not spread, as it could surely be traced back to her.

When Melissa came back for her next visit from Morehead, she was trim as ever and accompanied by a handsome coed. When she brought that boy to church, Janine just about dropped her teeth. It made Janine look like a fool when everyone saw Melissa looking so beautiful just months after Janine compared her to a sausage. Janine had on a cute pair of pink pumps that morning. Wonder if she thought about hurling one at Melissa?

Even though the rumor that Etta had innocently started had not spread, she still felt a need to do something kind for Melissa. That Sunday afternoon, she took the most beautiful china teacup to Melissa with the most touching handwritten note. The teacup was from Etta's collection that had been passed down from her mother. It was lavender, which matched the dress that Melissa had worn to church that morning. The note described how proud Etta was of Melissa and how much she had enjoyed watching her grow into a fine young lady. Melissa still treasures that teacup. After the whole incident, Etta vowed to never say another negative word about anybody, even to her husband.

Years later, Melissa's kindness forced Janine to burry the hatchet. After graduation, Melissa married that nice boy she brought to church. They moved back to Fletcher Hollow where they both got jobs teaching school. In the meantime, Janine wound up marrying Harris Jones. Harris grew up just two houses down from Janine. Janine was on the phone lamenting to her friend Opal. She was beginning to fear that she'd be an old maid and never realize her dream of having a child. Harris' momma, Ethel, picked up on that conversation and listened with intensity.

Harris had never had much luck with the ladies, but his momma thought he might have a chance with Janine. Ethel was itching to be a grandmother and was not above doing a little matchmaking. He turned out to be the catch of the century! During all those lonely days and nights, he'd been reading books about anything and everything. He educated himself on the business of buying and selling rare and antique glassware. Then, he started going to auctions and buying pieces. Before long, he had a valuable collection. Harris sent pictures of his collection to an auction house in New York City. I picked up one time when he was on the phone with the auction house and heard dollar amounts mentioned that absolutely blew my mind. Harris quickly reinvested the money and turned it over into a bigger fortune.

That man treats Janine like a princess! He coddles her and buys her anything she wants. Every season he sends her and

Barbara to Lexington to shop for clothes. A couple of years into the marriage, they had a beautiful baby boy. They named him Conrad, after Harris's great-grandfather. Motherhood and a happy marriage has softened Janine quite a bit. She's actually pretty sweet. As for Barbara, she's also become much more kind. Perhaps it's becoming a grandmother. More likely, it's that she's getting older and doesn't want to give St. Peter anymore sins for her list of transgressions.

When Conrad began kindergarten, Janine just about had a nervous breakdown. She did nothing but hover over him for five years and just couldn't bear to think of him being away from her all day. He wound up being placed in Melissa's class. On the first day of school, Janine tearfully dropped him off at the classroom door. Melissa went over to her, patted her on the shoulder, and promised to treat him well and make his first year of school enjoyable. And that's just what she did. Janine was so grateful for Melissa's treatment of Conrad that she came by the school early one day with a heartfelt apology for Melissa. From then on, the two got along splendidly.

A true friendship was solidified between them on one fateful October morning. The citizens of any mining town live with the near certainty that mining accidents will occur. Fletcher Hollow had been lucky. For ten years, nobody had died in the mine.

It was a crisp, cool October morning. The leaves were brilliant that year, setting the mountains ablaze in a thousand shades of orange, yellow, and red. It was Fall Carnival time. Janine had come to the school to help Melissa's class get ready for the festivities. That night, Conrad was to escort one of the Kindergarten princess candidates.

The kids were pressing leaves between sheets of waxed paper. Later they were planning to hang their leaf collections in the classroom windows. While Melissa carefully ran an iron over each leaf display, Janine showed the children how to wrap popcorn balls in brown butcher paper and tie them up with orange ribbon. The room was filled with excitement and anticipation.

Suddenly, their jovial mood was ceased by the sound of a blaring siren. The students did not know what was happening, because none of them had ever heard the siren. Janine and Melissa unfortunately knew all too well what it meant. When they were in sixth grade, the same sound pervaded Fletcher Hollow. It was a spring day and the kids were out of school for Good Friday. A section of the mine had caved in. Three miners lost their lives and one lost his leg. Life must go on after such tragedy, but the pain is never forgotten.

Little Tommy McGill, who has always been too smart for his own good yelled. "Something's happened down at the mine! My papaw's told me stories about that mine. When the siren goes off, somebody's been hurt real bad!"

More than half the kids in Melissa's class had daddies, and many of them grandfathers, working in the mine. As Melissa and Janine looked at the youngsters' panic-stricken faces, they grabbed hands and said a quick prayer. The prayer was silent; but as the women exchanged a teary glance, they knew that they were united in their faith. The principal came over the PA system, announcing that all children would be permitted to go home.

Melissa sent Janine to Mrs. Evan's and Mrs. Nolen's classrooms. Both of their husbands worked in the mine and they surely would want to go down there to check on the situation. Janine came back with all of the students from those rooms. The two women huddled with all of the children in a circle on the floor as relatives came by to pick them up. Not much was said, but hugs and prayers were exchanged through muffled sobbing. People in mining towns tend to be stoic, and this is passed on to the young. There were no questions of "why" or "what are we going to do." There was just an understanding that something bad had happened and that everyone would help each other through it.

Joe Carver was the last child to be picked up. Ella Duvall, his next-door-neighbor came to get him. The look on her face said it all. Joe's daddy hadn't survived. Ella had taken Joe's momma down to the mine after the alarm sounded. There had been an explosion in one section of the mine. The whole crew that Joe's dad was working with was killed. Joe's momma wanted to tell him herself, so Ella planned to fix Joe lunch and try to keep him busy until his momma could pull herself together.

In all, five men lost their lives that day. There wasn't a person in Fletcher Hollow who wasn't affected by the tragedy. For quite some time party line etiquette was ignored. Many tearful conversations were interrupted by people who didn't even need to make a call. They just yearned to hear another voice.

The good ladies of Fletcher Hollow came through for each other. Many of us got busy in our kitchens, making chocolate cakes and deviled eggs to take to families of the deceased. I stepped up my pecan pie production to three pies per week. Etta chose about a dozen of her prized china teacups to give to special friends who'd lost someone. In each cup was a little slip of paper with an encouraging Bible verse carefully printed on it. Most of all, we were just there for each other.

One week after the accident, a memorial service was held for the miners. The service ended with one of the greatest hymns ever written. As we sang "Blessed Be the Ties that Bind" hands and hearts were intertwined all through the sanctuary. Progress will come slowly to Fletcher Hollow and forever change the way things are done. For now the "tie that binds" a group of us ladies in town will be the party line.

Kori E. Frazier

Blackberry Spring

Lying awake in the tiny bedroom at the back of the small, white house we shared for the last years of my childhood, I would hear the creak of the door as my father returned from work late at night. His boots made heavy footfalls as he walked into the kitchen, where my mother would be sitting dutifully at the table, a pair of knitting needles or a torn dress in hand. I would try to fall asleep to the hum of their voices, but my excitement would ultimately be too intense to quell, for Daddy was home.

I would fling aside my quilt and hurry into the kitchen, the dirty floor rough against my bare feet. Mama raised her eyebrows in a forewarning glance accompanied by a reserved smile, while Daddy called out to me as I appeared in the doorway, the dynamic whites of his eyes and teeth accentuated against the blackness of his skin. Oh, he was white, with fiery red hair that on these nights was always dulled to the color of charred firewood accented by tiny specks of ember, but I didn't mind that he looked more like a dark skinned stranger than my father. I always knew it was him by the glimmer in his eyes as I jumped into his arms, my legs tight around his waist. I didn't mind that when I finally, reluctantly, pulled away, my muslin nightgown was covered with smudges of black soot. I didn't mind because he was my father, and I suppose my nine year old instinct knew that every night he came home alive was a gift from God.

Daddy began working for the Keystone Coal and Coke Company before I can remember; and, even now, looking back from a vantage point of more than a decade, it is hard for me to piece together the torn scraps of my past: a wooden cabin with a wide porch shaded by towering yellow poplars, Mama seated in a rocking chair, bathed in beams of sunlight filtering through their leaves, Daddy working the fields with a tired smile on his face, my older brother Charlie and I picking blackberries in the woods, our faces covered in bittersweet juice as more went into our mouths than our baskets. When I was old enough to ask about what happened to us, and receive an answer that was not sugarcoated with lies, Mama told me that the place I so dimly recall was our home until I was six. When I conjure up those brief, misty recollections, I can see Mama and Daddy's faces gleaming with contentment, hear my brother's wild laughter, and feel the warmth of their love permeate my body. I know that although those days were momentary and now so intangible, we were happy then.

And then came the man from the north.

Mama told me that she was taken in by his enthusiasm. She said he looked handsome and striking in his tweed suit and tie, the charismatic rise and fall in his voice tempting her. The man told her if Daddy would sell him his land, he'd give them two dollars an acre and nothing would change; the land, the house, the poplars would still be ours, and they would even give Daddy a good job in exchange for the use of our property. I have often thought that if it had been me, I would have refused him because it sounded too good a proposition to be true. But it was more money than we had, and so Daddy told him yes.

And it was just as he had promised. We still lived in the cabin; and although Daddy worked from early in the morning until late in the evening, we had money to feed the four of us without worrying about making do each day. Based on my limited remembrance, we were living the best we ever had, thanks to the nice man who came out of nowhere to pay us for simply doing what we'd always done.

A year later, the coal company forced us off our land.

They moved us from the mountain home my folks had made for us from the day they were married to the company town of Keystone, West Virginia, a barren plot of land where the miners' families were treated as unwanted baggage, and their sons were raised like cattle until their time came to be slaughtered in the shadows below the earth. We lived in a white, clapboard house that was but one of hundreds like it. We were given worthless paper to be used as money for the company store. Charlie and I learned to read and write in a company owned schoolhouse. Even the church was built with company wood, and the bells were purchased with the company money. And our bodies? The company owned them, too.

For three years, they owned my father, for seven months, they owned my brother; and until the day I die, they will own me.

* * * * *

That morning was beautiful and sunny, the kind that brings such delight to those who have endured the chill and bitterness of a hard winter. As I dressed and walked down our house's front steps for school, I was riveted by the shining blue sky and daffodils growing out of the wet, green grass that just weeks ago was brown and dead. I thought of Charlie, who had gone down the black hole for the first time just a year ago, and how as I breathed the flowery air, he knelt in pitch black, dying a little each day as his lungs grew caked with coal dust. I wished he could see what I saw. I still do.

As I walked, I struggled to balance my books with the lunch tin Mama had prepared for me, a bottle of milk and a piece of blackberry pie, accidentally dropping my books in the dirt. When I bent down to pick them up, I raised my head to see Mama standing on the front porch looking back at me, smiling. Her dark hair tousled in a messy bun and a knit shawl pulled tight around her shoulders, she hummed "The Green Rolling Hills of West Virginia" as she felt the cool air envelop her.

"You get on to school now, Llewellyn," she called; and, for a moment, her eyes seemed to glitter in the sunshine.

We learned arithmetic that morning. I remember my teacher Miss Evans's plain, blue cotton dress and white sweater, and the way the gold cross around her neck twirled on its chain as she scrawled problems on the blackboard. Our one room school-house was frozen in silence as we did our morning exercises; occasionally, the dead air would be broken by the tip of a pencil cracking or a student's cough or sneeze. It was the calm before the storm.

The door burst open.

"Miss Alice!"

Our heads turned as two men burst into the room. They were both dressed in dirty overalls and stopped in the doorway, sweat pouring down their faces in tearlike drops as they leaned on their knees to catch their breath.

Miss Evans stared at them, hands on her hips, her face somewhere between aggravated and distressed by their presence.

"Reece, what in the world do you want? We're in the middle of class and . . . "

"Miss Alice!" One of the two men stood up straight, having regained his composure, eyeing our teacher with marked distress. You gotta send all the children home right away!"

Her face fell in recognition.

"Why?" Years later, I would look back and remember the color draining from her cheeks as she asked a question to which she already knew the answer.

"It's the mine!" he cried. There's been an explosion in Number Two!" Some of the older children gasped, seeming to freeze as his words registered. The rest of us, the ones too young to realize what they had heard, just looked at the men, looked at Miss Evans, and looked back to the men, wonderingly, unknowingly.

Miss Evans closed her eyes, her hands folded and pressed tight into her bosom. Her chin rose toward the ceiling, and she murmured something soft under her breath as though in prayer. A young woman set to graduate the next month entered the same meditative state, pressing her joined hands to her forehead as a tear spilled from her eyes. At last, our teacher opened her eyes and spoke to us.

"Class dismissed," she said somberly. "Go home to your families."

We got up from our desks, moving at our own paces. The younger children tagged each other and began to race down the steps outside, excited by the prospect of an afternoon of no school, while the praying girl and her friends stuck close together as they exited to the tune of soft sobs. As the class filed out of the schoolhouse, I contemplated what I should do. Since we were told to go home, I knew that I probably should. What I wanted to know was "why." On any other day, we would still be sitting there, doing our math exercises and primer readings. What was so different about today? As I left the classroom, I looked toward the front of the room at Miss Evans, who was sitting at her desk, toying with the cross around her neck as she hugged herself and cried, before stepping out the door.

As I walked down the dirt path, I noticed the same brilliant blue sky and luminous sunshine that I had been so entranced by. It all looked the same, but somehow, the warm spring air seemed colder. Next to the schoolhouse, a woman not much older than my mother was banging on the door of the church, then fell to the ground, overcome with tears when the pastor appeared on the front steps. Further down the path, a young girl holding a baby stood wrapped in the arms of an older woman whom I took to be her mother, embracing her as the child wept in anguish. In the distance, I saw a crowd of mothers, daughters, and sisters moving away from town in a dark mass.

"Llewellyn!" I heard a voice call my name and turned around to see Mama rushing toward me. She fell on her knees, pulling me close to her. Suddenly overcome with the fear she exuded, I clung to her, burying my head in the sleeve of her dress as she lowered her head to meet mine.

"Darlin', don't you worry any," she whispered. "It's gonna be all right. We'll go down there and your daddy and Charlie'll be there a-waitin' for us and we'll . . . "

Her voice broke, and I felt my forehead grow damp.

She took a deep breath and got to her feet, taking my hand and gripping it tightly as we began the longest journey of our lives. Years later, I would recall the simple child I was then, walking with her mother toward a destination that was then nameless. I would remember the faces of the women walking with us, dark, icy eyes open in disbelief or closed in prayer and tears, appearing deep and sunken against their ashen skin.

"Mama, what . . . "

"Shhh, darlin', don't say a word." She squeezed my hand tighter, and I could feel the pulse hammering beneath her cold skin.

At last, a wooden mine shaft and its scaffold appeared in view, looming over the tops of the pines. Immediately, our pace quickened. I remember the faces of hundreds of women and children, still clear in my memory though their names have been erased by time. Near us, a woman in a grey dress began to sob softly, swaying with each step, until she was unable to walk and had to be helped to her feet by another in the crowd. Each step was surreal. Once, I thought I was dreaming; but as we walked through the brush beneath the trees, my ankle was nicked by the thorns of a blackberry bush; and I knew when I failed to awaken that I was not.

There were hundreds of us, women overwhelmed with dread, and children gazing innocently at the towering structure before them. Could they know this was where their daddies disappeared every morning and returned in each day's early hours, barely recognizable from the coal dust that coated their faces? Did they realize that as they idly ground their shoes into the dirt, men were suffering hundreds of feet below?

I was one of them. I didn't. A young woman in a brown dress streaked with flour passed through the crowd. Her hair was tied back with a white handkerchief and she smelled of baby milk. As she turned to face the women before her, her glassy eyes scanned the sea of faces, resilient, but not unmoved by trepidation. Taking a deep breath, she opened her mouth to speak.

"The Lord!" Her voice cracked under the strain of emotion, and she gathered her strength before starting over. "The Lord is my Shepherd; I shall not want. He maketh me to lie down in green pastures; he leadeth me beside the still waters." Gradually, a chorus of voices joined in, and heads fell like receding waves as they bowed in prayer.

Mama's hand began to tremble in mine.

"He restoreth my soul: He leadeth me in the paths of righteousness for His name's sake."

An icy gloom began to rise like a flood in my body, chilled blood throbbing and flowing behind my ears. I felt as though I should cry, but I couldn't. Only a few moments remained until life as I had known it slipped beyond my grasp.

Our voices rose in a quaking unison.

"Yea, though I walk through the valley of the shadow of death, I will fear no evil: for thou art with me; thy rod and thy staff."

A grave man came out the door of a tiny building next to the shaft.

An invisible dam broke. Women rushed the figures that stood before us, some stoic and quiet, others sobbing uncontrollably, all begging for answers in their own way.

He did not say a word, but gazed at us mournfully, and shook his head.

* * * * *

The eight coffins were laid in out in a straight, unwavering row; a pine box for each of the men killed in the Keystone mining disaster of 1928, though little remained of them but charred, indistinguishable bones. I did not go with Mama to say goodbye to Daddy and Charlie, but I know that she returned home that afternoon looking like a ghost back from the dead, her eyes bloodshot and bright against her pale skin. She went to bed as soon as she arrived and refused to come out; she did not attend the funeral; and I went in her stead. I placed daffodils on their graves and watered them with my tears.

An hour after the funeral, a man from the coal company knocked on the door of the white, clapboard house we had been forced into after being taken from our home. My father was dead, he said, and could no longer provide his services to Keystone.

"What do you mean?" Mama had asked him, though the heaviness I saw in her eyes indicated that she already knew it too well.

"It means," he replied coldly, "that if your husband can no longer provide for us, then we cannot continue to provide for you."

For the second time in three years, the Keystone Coal Company made us homeless.

We persevered in every way we knew, even though our survival meant leaving the mountains, the only home we had known. Mama got a job working in a textile factory up north in Ohio; and together, we went to Dayton, where buildings towered over us under a cinder colored sky. But just as the song she sang to me in my childhood says, "The green rolling hills of West Virginia will keep me and never let me go."

It was the land I was raised on; the land on which Daddy built the cabin for my mother in the forest of yellow poplars that still thrives in sweet, brief stills in my memory. It was the land where I would jump into his arms and have my nightgown smudged with coal when he came home at night. But it was also the land that was used to kill my family, and that can never be forgiven. It took away my Daddy, and it took Charlie long before his time, all in the name of progress.

As our nation thrived, my family died. And still, I can't let go.

Susan Noe Harmon

Secrets in the Cedar Chest

Molly's trip along the winding two-lane mountain road proved effortless. She traveled the familiar highway countless times visiting her grandmother. Several months passed since she relaxed on Grandma Sara's front porch. As the memories flooded her mind with a mixture of joy and sorrow, she felt an overwhelming desire to keep on driving and never look back. But then again, Grandma gave her a last mission; and she must see it through.

Nestled in a narrow holler deep in the Appalachian mountains of Kentucky, Grandma Sara's small five-room house displayed deterioration from the harsh inclement winters. Molly's father spoke often of his youthful days warming his hands near the potbelly stove in the drafty front room. Molly chuckled aloud as she recalled the day that the old iron monstrosity was replaced with baseboard electric heat. Her father and Grandma argued for years about it until Grandma finally agreed to this major change in her house; and, although the new warmth felt welcoming on a cold winter day, Grandma frequently spoke of her old reliable coal stove as if it were a deceased family member.

As the rain pelted on the frosty windshield of Molly's old truck, she thought, "Why didn't I have that heater repaired? I'm glad Daddy insisted that I wear warm clothes but I'll never admit it to him. Darn, I forgot my gloves!" Her fingers numbed around the frigid steering wheel.

Earlier that morning, Molly's father gave her a sealed envelope, addressed to her in Grandma's handwriting.

"Molly, this is for you from Grandma," her father said. His dark blue eyes were still swollen, teary from the funeral services the previous day. "Honey, she said for you to open the letter at her house, not before. Do you want me to go with you?" His voice trembled as he placed the letter in Molly's delicate hand.

"No, Daddy, I want to go by myself. I have to do this. I'm takin' my cell phone an' I shouldn't be there very long. I'll be back before dark, I promise," Molly replied.

She really didn't want her father to accompany her. Wrapping her arms around her father's neck, she gave him a peck on the cheek. His face mirrored a sad lonely child. Never seeing her father in such disarray, it scared her. When Grandpa died 10 years ago, and then again when Molly's mother unexpectedly passed away, it was Daddy who took charge. Oh, Daddy! It's just you an' me now, she thought. What are we goin' to do?

Molly's warm breath fogged the view as she turned into her grandmother's driveway. As the temperatures sharply dropped, the rain changed to sleet so quickly that she nearly fell on the icy porch steps. The wooden porch swing, swaying by the bitter cold wind, flashed a comforting memory of her days with Grandma. She recalled the wonderful summer afternoons they spent in that old swing enjoying the scent of honeysuckle and lilac, the peacefulness of the holler. Most of all they enjoyed each other's company.

Shivering, Molly fumbled with the door key for several minutes before entering the dark lonely house. "Grandma, it's me!" she yelled. "It's Molly!" She just wanted to say it one last time.

Never alone in Grandma's house before, she turned the lights on in every room. "Everything's the same an' everything's different," she thought. "It's too quiet."

Laying her coat and hat over the couch, she shook her long dark unruly hair and glanced in the living room mirror. "Grandma, I don't know if I can stay here an' do this. I'm not strong like you. What am I goin' to do without you? You're my other Mother an' now you're gone," she thought. With her finger, she traced the outline of her face in the mirror. "I really do look like my Grandma!"

Age never hindered the relationship between Molly and her grandmother. They enjoyed an occasional debate, usually ending in hysterical laughter. Molly trusted Grandma with her youthful adventures and her troubles as a young adult. Grandma rarely talked about herself, except for a couple of family tales. Grandma's gift of listening provided Molly with a comforter of love. Now she would feel a chill without it.

The sleet continued to plummet, the skies darkened early. Ice pellets covered the yard, the majestic pines glistened. Any other time Molly relished the idea of staying the night at Grandma's house, but this time dread consumed her. She turned on the porch light. From the window she looked out on a spectacular winter wonderland.

I need to call Daddy she thought. Rummaging her purse, a delightful memory of an intense conversation with her grandmother brought a loud giggle in the midst of the unexpected chaos. She recalled fondly how Grandma used to say, "Honey, you don't need a contraption like that. It ain't natural. Those things will be the ruination of society! Won't last long, I'll tell you that! Why, it ain't a real telephone anyway. It looks like you're talkin' to a ghost!" As a very young girl, Molly learned not to contradict Grandma, on anything—ever. But occasionally, she enjoyed getting Grandma riled up.

Quickly, she dialed her cell phone. "Daddy, it's terrible up here! The ice covered everything, even the trees, an' its snowing awfully hard! I'm goin' stay here tonight. Don't worry. It's better than gettin' out in this mess!"

"Oh, Molly, I'm so sorry," Daddy apologized. "I should've come with you! Don't try to drive. It's not safe an' I don't know what I'd do if I lost you too! You're all I've got!"

"Daddy. I'm just fine. I'll call you in the morning. Please try to rest," Molly said in her meager attempt to console him. One thing at a time, one thing at a time. I'll take care of Daddy tomorrow, she told herself.

As Molly ended the call, she heard a loud crackle and thundering boom. She opened the door to see a large tree limb lying over her truck bed. I couldn't leave here now if I wanted to! The weight of the ice snapped a large branch from the towering oak, spoiling another precious memory of her childhood. Long ago, Grandma fashioned a tire swing for her, and even all grown up, Molly continued to enjoy the swing under the coolness of that tree in the summers. Once, Molly caught Grandma in the swing, artfully kicking her feet to go higher, her dress flapping in the breeze, and a playful smile on her face. This confirmed Molly's suspicion that her Grandma knew how to do everything.

Molly felt out of control, her world crumbling. I want my Grandma! This ain't fair! She slammed the door and locked it, rattling the tiny ceramic figures that showcased Grandma's glass curio cabinet. Her grandmother fussed at her beyond count for slamming the front door, instilling a real fear of someday breaking every one of her prized figurines. Annoyed with herself and everything else Molly threw up her hands, walked into the kitchen, and grabbed a glass of water.

"Oh, my gosh! It's still here. I can't believe it!" she said aloud. Her fingers followed the etching of a tiny house that she carved into the wooden kitchen table as a small child. "I forgot all that. I don't think she ever told Mama or Daddy," she thought. Smiling down at the deep marks made by a forbidden paring knife, she realized her grandmother was a keeper of memories. Although a fruit bowl or tablecloth often covered the jagged artwork, Grandma never complained.

Molly laid the white envelope on the table, staring at it for several minutes. A definite imprint of a key inside the letter captured her curiosity. Taking a deep breath, she ripped open the mystery envelope, and began her journey. As she read the letter, she clutched an old tarnished skeleton key in her right hand.

My Dearest Molly,

The key unlocks the cedar chest in my bedroom. It was my intention to complete a family tree for you to have someday, but I soon discarded the idea. Everybody is born, and everybody dies. Statistics tell nothing about a person or how they lived. My dear grandchild, for you to appreciate the woman you are, you need to know from where you came. Your Daddy will tell you of his childhood and the generation of his era. But it is important for you to know something about your Appalachian family many years ago. Among various and interesting articles inside the chest, you will find a scrapbook, giving you some insight as to how we lived, loved, struggled, and celebrated life and death. My hope is that you keep these stories close to your heart. Pass them to your children so that our spirit will continue to play a part in their lives too. Your legacy awaits. Please know that I loved you from the first time I touched your tiny hands. I will always be with you because we are family.

Grandma Sara

Images flooded Molly's mind. She rubbed her eyes fiercely, attempting to erase the pain and fill an undeniable void forced into her life. She shoved the letter back in the envelope and threw it in the floor. Staring at the key, still unaware that her world was about to merge with history, anger rose like a sleeping giant. How dare she leave me! "Grandpa! Mama! Is there somethin' wrong with me?" Nothing prepared her for the intense emotions consuming entire being, the pain she carefully avoided for so many years.

Grandma's bedroom was untouched. Her massive feather bed, covered with a Dutch Girl quilt, displaying the tiny hand stitching of her grandmother's talent. On her dresser lay three items: a beautiful silver brush and comb, and a bottle of Oil of Olay. Molly smiled as she remembered Grandma saying, "Hide your toiletries in a drawer. No lady shows her make-up in plain sight. It's only proper."

Once again, the cedar chest at the end of the bed aroused the young woman's curiosity. Although Molly made untold efforts to open the chest when she was younger, now, she was the owner, the possessor of the key to Grandma's secrets and treasures. She felt honored.

She sat down on the small embroidered footstool beside the chest. Gathering her wits, she unlocked the chest and raised the lid slowly, allowing the aroma of the cedar to permeate the room. Inside the chest, several articles of old clothing lay neatly to the side. A small mink collar wrapped in a plastic bag nestled in a corner along with a tiny pair of yellowed white lace gloves covered in tissue paper. I can't ever remember Grandma wearing fancy things like this! Molly laid them on the bed. Carefully, she removed a pair of thin beaded moccasins, mindful of its age. At last! she thought, pulling a scrapbook out of the chest and settling comfortably in her grandmother's bed. The large goose down pillows nearly swallowed Molly, leaving her to wonder, "I'm surprised Grandma didn't get lost in this bed, as little as she was!" Opening the scrapbook, she found a note tucked neatly in the crease of the first page.

My Dearest Grandchild,

Enjoy these photographs and written accounts of your ancestry, especially of your great great great great great-grandmother, Ahyoka Clark. Some of the stories have been kept alive only by word of mouth, possibly giving way to some exaggeration. Nevertheless, this is your family. Be proud.

Love, Grandma

Molly heard the frozen tree branches beat against the bedroom window. She pulled the quilt up over her legs. It seemed nature insisted that the young woman give her full attention to the impending revelations. "Okay, Grandma, let's see what is so important," she thought.

Turning the page, her eyes fixed on an old faded photo of a little woman sitting on a wooden porch holding a small spotted dog. Somewhat attractive, her sharp facial features made it difficult to determine her age. Her deep-set eyes were hauntingly sad. She wore moccasins. Yet, it was the woman's exceedingly long white hair that held her attention. Unfolding the handwritten story, Molly began to read.

In the spring of 1838, John Clark, a local farmer, came upon a beautiful Cherokee maiden, Ahyoka, as she washed clothes in the river. Alone, embarrassed, and somewhat afraid of the stocky man holding a Kentucky rifle, she ran into the woods, leaving the wet clothes in her basket. Quickly, he followed, catching her as she stumbled, both landing in a patch of ivy.

"Wait a darn minute, will you! I ain't goin' to hurt you!" John hollered as he tried to keep the wild young girl's fists away from his face. "You 're goin' to beat me to death!"

"Leave me!" she screamed. Her swift kick into his stomach caused the man to wish he stayed at home that day.

As John rolled in the lush poison ivy, he groaned, "You left your wash at the river. That's all I wanted to tell you."

"Oh! I'm so sorry," Ahyoka mumbled. She searched his deep blue eyes, deciding there was no threat. Offering her hand, he stood up.

"You pack a pretty good punch," he said. "I'll bet you have many brothers."

"I have eight brothers. I know how to fight!" she answered as she lifted the flintlock out of the brush. "Here is your rifle! Now leave me!"

As he reached for his weapon, he was suddenly mesmerized by her beauty, her eyes of liquid brown, her long flowing black hair, the nimbleness of her body. Blood rushed to his brain so swift he nearly fainted. "I didn't mean to scare you. My name is John Clark an' I got a farm on the other side of the river down in Cumberland Gap. I was up this way checkin' traps an' just ran into you. I didn't mean no harm, truly," he said, struggling with every word.

Ahyoka nodded, accepting his apology. She turned, running back for her basket. Her father fretted when she dawdled. Later that night, she lay thinking about this new man and the many reasons to forget about him. But she couldn't forget him or the poison ivy.

Days passed without another chance meeting. The wash days increased as she hoped to see her John Clark. Her family, pleased with the sudden interest in washing clothes, never imagined the fifteen year old girl had a secret love. She held an honorable standing in the tribal community, largely due to her father, a proud medicine man.

Failing to erase her from his mind, John succumbed to the realization that he wanted this woman. He knew the seriousness of his decision, condemned with no future in the white or the Indian communities. His farm offered her food and shelter. His heart offered love and devotion.

Three weeks to the day, his rash healed, John returned to the river. And as if a repeat of the first encounter, he startled Ahyoka, this time so much she slipped on a rock, falling into the river. He jumped into the water, thinking surely she would drown.

"If you don't let go of me, I'm goin' to hit you!" she yelled, pushing him away. "You're goin' to have to quit scarin' me if we're goin' keep on meetin'." Getting her bearings, she stood up in the waist deep river.

"Woman, I was only tryin' to save you! Don't be hittin' on me all the time. A body can only take so much. I'm a peaceful man 'til I'm riled," he warned in frustration.

As he stood up in front of her, he knew he was defeated. Suddenly, the drowned rat cupped the face of the beautiful nymph in his calloused hands, gently kissing her on the forehead. It was so unexpected that both of them jerked backward, falling again into the water. They laughed.

Helping her out of the water onto the bank, they sat side by side, the warm sun drying their soaked clothing. "I don't even know your name," he said. He didn't look at her, afraid she could see inside his heart.

"My name is Ahyoka. In your world, it means 'she brought happiness.' Your name is John Clark. You see, I remembered!"

He turned to see the most beautiful woman smiling at him. "You know this is forbidden. If you leave now, I'll try to forget you . . . but I cannot promise," he whispered. His heart pounded so loud he barely heard her reply.

She looked directly into his eyes. "I will not leave you."

Yet, it was the unsaid words that formed their bond. For months, they met often at the river. They talked, laughed, played, stealing every precious moment. If caught, he knew the shame cast upon her family crushed their rank within the tribe. Aware that her existence in a white man's society proved unacceptable to most of the townspeople, he carefully planned their meetings. For himself, he didn't care. He loved her. Ahyoka prepared for her parent's wrath if her tryst was discovered. She loved him.

Late in September, the tribe prepared to leave, joining others for the long journey to Oklahoma. She had not met with her John for two weeks because of the disruption within the camp. Her heart was broken. Her sadness went unnoticed.

When gold was discovered in Georgia, the Indian treaty was declared null and void, leading to a most shameful land-grab and ultimately the horrific death march of the Cherokee, now called "The Trail of Tears." Although the Cherokee roundup began in May of 1838, for most Cherokee, the exodus began later that year. They put up a strong resistance and were among the last evicted of their homeland.

The day before the tribe gathered to leave, John Clark entered the camp on horseback. Head held high, he sought out the home of Ahyoka. Clearly unwelcome, especially under the circumstances, he was determined to approach her family and extend an offering. As he dismounted his horse in front of the log cabin, her father came out on the porch.

"What do you want?" the father asked defiantly. He had no time for idle talk.

"I am John Clark. I know your daughter, Ahyoka. I want to take her to my home," he said. "I am a good man." The words spilled out of his mouth.

Shocked by this revelation, the father told John to wait as he went back into the cabin. An eternity passed before the father returned and motioned John to come into their home. Once inside, Ahyoka's mother confronted him sharply.

"Mr. Clark, how do you know my daughter?" her mother asked. Ahyoka stood between her parents, stunned by John's bravery.

"I saw her at the river. Since then we have met many times. I do not want her to leave. I love her," he explained.

The mother rolled her eyes and shook her head. "Ahyoka, how well do you know this man?"

"I love him, mother."

"Daughter, do you see . . . he is bald!" her mother exclaimed.

"I don't care! He is mine!"

Her mother leaned in closer to John's face as a ploy to intimidate him. "Mr. Clark! You are old!" she shouted.

"Ma'am, I have 10 acres of the richest soil east of the Mississippi, a barn full of healthy livestock, and a strong back. I am old enough to provide for your daughter, but still young enough to give her many children. I can assure you that she will be safe," John stated with an air of confidence.

Reluctantly, Ahyoka's parents agreed for her to stay with this baldheaded old man who professed his undying love for their daughter. They chose the lesser of the two evils with hope that at least one of their children might have a long and prosperous life.

"Go! Go tonight, my child. Your brother will walk your side to the river to meet this John Clark," her mother announced.

"You have our blessing," her father interjected. "We will always be with you." Staring at the man who was going to take his daughter, her father spoke slowly, "Do not hurt her!" Everyone felt her father's powerful energy as if a lightening strike was imminent. John nodded his head.

Late that night, Ahyoka kissed her family goodbye, and with her oldest brother, walked away from the camp for the last time. She did not look back. John was waiting for them as they approached the small clearing near the river. She kissed her sibling farewell and sent him back to camp.

"Please, don't cry," John whispered. He cradled her until her brother's shadow disappeared into the woods.

"I'm not cryin' for myself, I'm cryin' for my family," she said, wiping her tears. She clutched her small bag of belongings. "Hurry! Let's go."

Ahyoka never saw her family again. News spread rampantly of the thousands dead from the forced relocation. Fearful of her discovery, John kept Ahyoka hidden on his farm until April 1839 after the last of the tribes reached Oklahoma. During the winter months, John took her as his common law wife. No clergy performed a marriage ceremony between an Indian and a white man in that area, so they dedicated their lives to God and to each other on Thanksgiving Day. He taught her about scripture, she taught him of the harmony and balance in the realm of the earth. It was a learning process for both of them during those months while she hid from the rest of the world.

On a spring day, John drove the buckboard into town with his new bride by his side. The incessant wagging tongues caused major confusion inside the stores and especially the courthouse. Intentional snubbing and the openly vicious chatter did not deter John from walking proudly down the sidewalk with his lovely wife. As John completed his business in the local hardware store, a bolt of fabric captured Ahyoka's attention. She touched the soft cloth, rubbing a piece against her cheek.

"Don't do that!" the store clerk screamed. "You'll get it dirty!"

Startled, Ahyoka jumped. "I'm sorry."

John, observing the incident, took the material to the counter. "Give me three yards of this cloth for my wife! Put it on my account!" he ordered.

"Are you sure you know what you're doin', John?" the clerk asked.

"Of course, I do!"

The typical attitude of the townspeople failed to change for many years. By the time Ahyoka was in her middle twenties, she had birthed four healthy children, two boys and two girls. She home-schooled the children, attempting to shield them from prejudice and ignorance. In addition to the household chores, she worked beside her husband tending the crops, fencing the pasture, and feeding the livestock. Their home was simple but comfortable. Occasionally, she yearned for an extra room or two but the bank continued to refuse her husband a loan. "I'm to blame," she thought. Nevertheless, the family led happy lives in social isolation until fate dealt a cruel and lasting blow.

By 1863, three of the children had left the nest. The older son, Joseph, built a house on the family property. The other son moved near Franklin, Tennessee and joined the Confederate Army under General Hood. Sadly, Ahyoka never heard from him again. The older daughter, Wenona, married a drunkard, moved across the Tennessee border, finally settling at the foot of Black Mountain in Harlan County, Kentucky. This caused Ahyoka and John many sleepless nights. Mysteriously, her daughter's husband was found dead, stuffed in a horse trough, his head detached from his body. The local doctor, familiar with the violent man, ruled the death a suicide. It was never questioned. The second daughter, Mary, continued to live at home.

In the summer of 1864, a drought set in, causing hardship on every living creature. The crops suffered; the livestock thinned; and dirt seeped into the well water. John rode out to the pasture to check on the cattle. As the sun blazed, John's vision became distorted. He failed to see the large copperhead in his horse's path. The spooked horse reared up causing John to fall off, hitting his head on a rock. He died instantly. In late afternoon, Ahyoka found his horse back in the barn. She knew something terrible happened to her husband. When she found him, she laid herself on his sunburned body and wailed for hours. Her sorrow echoed throughout the mountains. Before dusk, two neighbor men rode up, investigating the sounds. They helped her take John's remains back to the house. Ahyoka walked behind the horse that carried her husband's lifeless body. Devastated, Mary, cried uncontrollably, unable to be of any use to her mother. The men began digging the grave behind the house near a tall oak tree, working by moonlight until exhausted. They returned the next day, finishing the job before noon. Ahyoka and Mary buried their loved one as the clouds burst open. They stood at the grave site, soaked, the rain covering their tears.

"Our love began at a river many years ago. Now I say good-bye to you in rain. We were bound by life's nourishment," Ahyoka cried. "I will see you again, John Clark."

Relieved when the neighbor men refused her offer of pay, she graciously thanked them for their services. They tipped their hats and left. Later that afternoon, son Joseph returned from a hunting trip. Shocked and distraught from the news, he spent hours under the oak tree in the rain to be near his father. He left before daybreak.

Early that morning, Mary called into her mother's room, "I think I'll visit father before I do my chores!" Not hearing a response, she stepped in the bedroom, finding Ahyoka sitting at her vanity. Mary screamed, "Mother, what happened to your hair?" She ran to her and caressed her mother's long flowing hair—now white as snow.

"It came over night," Ahyoka said weakly, staring in the mirror. "Do not worry."

Ahyoka, passed away on Thanksgiving Day, four months after her husband was laid to rest. Three of her children were by her bedside as she prepared them for her death. "Do not mourn for me. Your father an' I will always be with you." She closed her eyes. The official cause of death was fever, although, some said she died of a broken heart.

Molly awoke as daylight filled the room. Rubbing her eyes, she saw the scrapbook still in her lap. I must've been exhausted! "It looks like I never moved," she thought. Crawling out of the bed, she stumbled into the kitchen and turned on the radio. I'll put a pot of coffee on. She gazed out the window. "The salt truck! I see the salt truck!" She grabbed her coat and ran outside to meet the driver as he was getting out of the truck.

"Hey, are you Molly?" the driver hollered. He removed his toboggan from his face.

"Yes! Why?"

"The name's Bill. Your daddy called the county garage this morning to see when we'd be up this way. He's worried. I figured I'd come an' check on you. The roads are still slick," he explained as he pulled the tree limb off the truck. "Do you need a lift out of here?"

"Thanks but I'll be fine now," she said. As she reached for the door handle she lost her balance. Trying to break her fall, Bill grabbed her coat, causing both to fall.

"Get off of me!" Molly shouted, flailing her arms.

"I ain't on you! I was tryin' to catch you from fallin'! Are you always this grateful?"

"Yeah! Sometimes I'm almost nice!" Molly replied sarcastically. *What's wrong with me? I don't act like this!* She stood up and shook the snow off her clothing. Ashamed, she offered her hand. "Come on! I'll help you up!"

"No thanks! You're dangerous, woman!"

"Suit yourself," Molly said, heading back inside the warm house.

"Would it hurt you to offer me a cup of coffee?" Bill asked as he followed her to the porch. *She was frustrating yet beckoning. He couldn't leave.*

"Fine. I've already got a pot made. Take your shoes off! Don't be makin' puddles in my Grandma's house!" she ordered.

They sat at the kitchen table in their sock feet sipping welcome steaming cups of coffee.

"What's this?" he asked, pointing at the carving in the table. "*She's so pretty that she's got me dumbfuzzled, he thought, probably wouldn't have anything to do with this old man anyway!*"

"Why, it's a drawing by a famous artist in the family!" she quipped without hesitation.

They laughed together. Molly felt a blush come over her as she thought, "He's cute!"

"I'm sorry about your grandmother," he said. "She was a good woman."

"How did you know her?"

"A few years back, my mother got a bad case of shingles. The doctor did all he could but she was in terrible pain. He told me to come see your grandmother, so I did. She gave me a black paste in a mason jar that smelled worse than rotten fish. Anyway, my mother used it, an' in less than two weeks, she was cured. I offered to pay your grandmother but she refused. I asked her if she studied medicine or somethin', an' she told me it was in her blood."

Molly smiled and thought, "That's right. That is so right!"

"Someday I would like to tell you about my grandmother and grandfather."

"Sounds like a story that would take awhile?"

As they looked into each other's eyes, he reached over and touched her hand.

P. J. Wilson

Mad Dogs

I watched him out of the corner of my eye to see if he was watching me. There was something about my brother that I did not trust. At five years of age I had not yet established my place in the family hierarchy, nor did I know if I were even allowed to have these feelings of mistrust about him. His place in my life had never been secure. Even though I knew that he was a part of us there was still something tentative about his relationship to the family, as if he had disgraced us somehow, or was expected to at any minute. He was fifteen years older than me, and had never lived in our house, or at least that is what I believed back then, but of course, my memory only stretched so far. Years later, after he died, I learned that he had run away to Norfolk to work in the shipyards during the war. According to my best estimation he must have been around twelve or thirteen then, but I cannot believe it possible that my parents would have let him go had they known. He came home on a Greyhound bus when the men returned to take up their old jobs.

However, he did not come back to our house until the night that Mama got sick. I woke up and heard the commotion downstairs, but drifting in and out of sleep the way a child does I held on to the belief that whatever misfortune was about to come into our lives would just as soon go away. A rim shard of a yellow moon had escaped into the room and it worked its way into the design of the crazy quilt on my bed. My eyes followed its shimmering light across the quilt, over the edge of the footboard and down the stairs to where he was standing on the ledge that separated the upstairs from the downstairs. My father had built this section onto the house — the log house that had been built by my great-great grandfather in 1838 — and so it had a constant look about it of being unfinished, as if we were living in a tree house. As it turned out it was never finished. One moment I had been asleep: and the next he was there, bending over the bed, waking Sissy, whispering softly to her. "Time to get up," he said.

In my sleepy state I mistook him for the monster that occasionally lived under my bed. But Sissy jumped into his arms whooping with delight. I hung back, studying him for the obvious flaws that I knew to be in his character. "Don't you want to give your old brother a hug?" he asked me. I shook my head. "I'll carry you downstairs on my back," he offered.

I knew he was trying to bribe me because something bad had happened, and I remember this as the exact moment when I began to associate him with *any* impending doom, as if he had caused it by coming home. Even after I learned that it was not his fault, and that Mama was never going to get well, I still held it against him, and was never quite able to forgive him for ruining our lives.

"No," I said, backing away, and fell against the bed into the moon and the crazy quilt. Sissy jumped on his back anyway and began to whistle as if he were her trick pony. She was such a tomboy. I followed them because I was afraid to stay in the room by myself, but all the while I watched them, their two hulking shadows form a hunchbacked hippogriff in the gathering light on the stairwell. The apparition preceded me down the stairs, two steps in front, but never far enough ahead that the monster behind me, the one that lived in the upstairs room, could overtake me alone and defenseless on the stairway, nor close enough to be lost in their merging shadows. The constant fears that would plague me for all of my life were then still forming, yet they had become grounded somehow in a mysterious dream that God had warned me even before my birth that there would be danger everywhere. As if He had, in fact, whispered in my ear just before the moment of birth that in this world I would eventually be taken down by an innocuous sounding term called friendly fire. I followed them down the stairs and had a premonition of this dream.

He made an apron for me from tissue paper and taught me how to stand on a chair and cut biscuits out of dough with a drinking glass. "I couldn't make breakfast without you," he teased, and Sissy laughed.

She was pouring beaten eggs into an iron skillet over the wood stove. "What about me?" she asked.

"You too," he said. "You're the woman of the house now."

He had brought two hunting dogs home with him when he came that night and had warned me never to play with them. "They're only for hunting," he said.

But I would sneak them out when he wasn't around and teach them how to be my dogs. The day the dog bit me he had been out hunting and came back across the field with the shotgun, broken breech, flung over his shoulder. The two dogs lagged behind him, their hips rolling into the ground as they walked. He went into the house and hung the gun over the door, and stood there in the doorway looking down at the dogs.

I came up behind the blue tick one and put my arms around him as I had done a million times before. I wanted to show him that I had tamed the dogs. The dog's head lolled forward in slow motion like some dumb lummox. He yipped once, a terrible sound, and bit me on the forehead. Slobber rolled down my face as the double-crossing dog cast his sorrowful eyes back to his master. "I told you not to play with them," he said sharply.

I moaned and pretended to faint, but I could still see him through my half-open eyelashes. Mama was standing in the doorway now looking at us. He came down the steps then all concerned. "Did he bite you?" he asked.

I did not answer. By now I was in a full-blown swoon. My hand held onto the place where the dog had bit me, but I managed to roll my eyes back into my head as my knees seemed to buckle under, and almost gracefully, I began to topple over. I timed my fall exactly to the point when he was there to catch me. I had learned this trick several months earlier when I was playing on the top of a stump while Daddy was cutting firewood. I had leaned forward to watch the ax come down and just as I did I saw the look of horror on Daddy's face as he tried to stop it from coming down into the back of my head. I fell off of the stump and began to run toward Daddy; at least I thought I was running toward him. But in my confusion I was running in the opposite direction. Before I could make it around the fallen tree my world began to grow dark. I didn't remember anything else after that—but I did learn one important thing. A fainting child gets attention fast. I used this method throughout my entire childhood and well into my adult years. I got away with it because no one would challenge me. I had that old head wound to back me up.

Now my brother picked me up and carried me into the house and laid me down on Mama's bed. I began to come out of my deep pretend faint then. "You okay?" he asked.

"Yes," I moaned weakly.

He was clever and I could see through the tiny slits in my eyes that I had not fooled him. Even though he knew that I was just playacting I did not care. "I'll tie the dogs up," he told Mama.

She was washing my face with a wet washcloth and I pushed my body into hers as hard as I could, separating her from him.

All the rest of the day and through the night the dogs staggered around, yipped, puked, slobbered, and fell over as if their hips were paralyzed. Daddy said it was mad dog fever, and they would have to be destroyed and their heads sent off to Richmond.

The next day the dogs were fine, but Daddy still insisted that we had to know if it was rabies. "Do you want to do it, or do you want me to?" Daddy asked.

There was no arguing with him; the decision had been made. "I'll do it," my brother said.

He took them off then, walking slowly toward the barn, and the dogs followed behind him believing they were going hunting.

"Come in the house," Mama said, so I did not hear the gunshots.

"You tell me if you ever see a low flying plane," he told me the next day. "Sure," I said, not knowing why. Maybe they were looking for more mad dogs.

I had taken to wearing only my slip that summer. "Where's your dress?" he asked me one day as I followed him toward his car.

"I took it off," I told him.

He was going to see his girlfriend and Sissy wanted to go. "How do you know where I'm going?" he asked her.

He liked to be mysterious like that. I was already crawling into the back seat of his car. She could wait for an answer if she wanted to, but I figured it would be a lot harder to say no if I was already sitting in the car. Sissy sat in the front seat beside him. The driveway leading to our house was almost a mile long and there were three gates to be opened. They were not the easy to open kind either, but homemade "gaps", as we called them, made of barbed wire and thin poles. Sissy opened each one, struggling to stretch the barbed wire out into a straight line, and stood there beside the fence as we drove through. I waved to her each time.

I liked his girlfriend, Corrine, and wanted to go to her house. She never asked me stupid things like where was my dress. Instead she said, "You look cool today. I wish I could wear my slip."

"Y'awl go on back to the house now," he said, as Sissy opened the last gate. She got really mad at him then, but he said we couldn't go because I just had my slip on.

"All he wanted us to do was open the stupid gates," she said. "I can't believe he did that."

I could believe it. I had already begun my long career as a stoic by then and I wasn't surprised at anything. "I knew he wouldn't let us go," I said, but she just yelled at me and said it was my entire fault.

The warm sand of the driveway felt good on my feet and I didn't mind the walk. I watched the blue mountains in the distant and pretended that I was not going toward them, but that they were coming to me. Sissy fumed all the way back while I took secret pleasure in her angst. As I look back on it, I feel a sense of shame because now I can only recall her goodness. Each evening she took the lantern down from the shelf behind the water bucket, lit it—shaking out the match before the flame touched her fingers—and walked with me to the outhouse. There she stood patiently by while I grunted and groaned, distorting my young/old face into a complex map of controlled agony. As long as she stood beside me the monsters stayed away. This image of her grace was lost on me then as I judged her mercilessly for believing any concept more rock-solid than the sand squishing between our toes.

"What did you expect?" Mama asked when we got back to the house.

That's what I wanted to know. "I'm not going to tell him if I see any low flying planes," I said.

"Oh, shut up," Sissy said. "You don't even know what you're talking about."

The next day the low flying plane came. I watched it fly along the creek bed, over what we call "the Stone place," circling twice over Sycamore Creek, rising high into the sky and disappearing.

I went into the house, past Mama and Daddy, and up the stairs all by myself. In the middle of the room I gave a big leap over the monster that lived under the bed and landed in the middle of the unmade bed. I did not wake up until the next morning. I crept quietly down the stairs and I could hear Mama and Daddy talking. "I hope you are satisfied," she was saying.

"I had to do it," he said. "I couldn't take another chance with her. What if we'd lost another child?" he asked.

I knew this was not a question for me to answer so I backed slowly up the stairs, almost to the top of the landing and then bounded down again, hitting each stair with a loud thud so that they would hear me and stop talking about things that didn't concern me—little pitchers with big ears.

The gun that had been hanging over the doorway was no longer there. Apparently he was gone again.

Mama died when I was eight, still suffering from that mysterious affliction that had brought him home three years earlier. Daddy seemed to grieve away to nothing after that. He died two years later. My brother was married by then to a doe-eyed child-bride that got her words mixed up and said silly things that didn't make any sense. She was jealous of his old girlfriend and called Corrine "old chlorine" and did for the rest of her life. The aunts and uncles came in right away and started throwing our things out. They told us to pack our clothes. Sissy insisted that he would come to get us, that he would get a house big enough for all of us to live in, but I didn't see how. He lived with his mother-in-law because his wife was afraid of the dark and could not stay alone while he worked the night shift. Maybe she had monsters under her bed as well.

By then I was no longer afraid of monsters for I had learned that there were many things far worse. Things that would never touch you, but could leave a scar six inches deep. I had by then accepted Stoicism as my personal savior, and had begun collecting pictures of a suffering Christ on a blue cardboard background with quizzical sayings such as "Book of Life—Is my name written there?" The words were spelled out in silver glitter and glowed in the dark so that I could study them in the moonlight, and the image was burned in my psyche forever. I packed my clothes in a cardboard box and left the house with the aunts and uncles. The home that we left behind stayed empty until I turned twenty-one. I thought somehow that it would be waiting for me when I turned grown, but he inherited it, not me. I told him if he ever decided to sell it, to let me know. He did sell it within the year, but not to me. It went to a stranger who owns it even today. He speaks of it fondly as if it had been his homeplace; or else he just wants to annoy me. Occasionally I walk there and lay flowers on the graves of my departed family. I do not belong there anymore for the home-house has fallen into ruins. Not even a foundation remains.

I should not have judged Sissy so harshly back when we were children, for she stayed with me always, if not in reality at least in my memory. She held my head while the doctor pumped my stomach and her hand was icy cold across my forehead. She had trouble catching her breath and gasped for air several times. The doctor looked at her with more concern than he showed for me. He was a young doctor, newly come to the emergency room, and had no sympathy whatsoever for someone who would try to take her own life. As he handled me roughly she continued to ask why. "How could you do this?" she asked over and over. After I expelled all the poison from my stomach she finally convinced me that there was a world of bright sunlight waiting for me somewhere out there in that unquantified place called the future. But God help me now, if I had known then what lay ahead I would have swallowed another bottle of pills.

The aunts and uncles seemed to have drawn straws for us, and tired of us just as quickly. We moved from place to place, all the while Sissy insisting that he would come for us eventually. After awhile we became child-brides ourselves.

I married an awkward boy who treated me like chattel until I became even more weary and disjointed. After awhile I just slipped away to live in a different kind of world, one peopled by those of my own imagination.

Sissy remains happy and optimistic even to this day. Proving, I suppose, that life does hand us what we make of it.

I had known all along that he would never come, and even if he did I knew that I would not be able to live in that perfect world that Sissy had dreamed up in her head. Guilt or something worse would keep me away from him all the days of my life.

It was the dogs that gave him away back then. When the heads were sent off to Richmond, they discovered it wasn't rabies after all. The dogs were drunk on the run-off from a moonshine still that the revenuers had found over on the Stone place when they flew over it that long ago day in a low flying plane.

Susanna Holstein

Gracie's Cabin

Folks who first settled West Virginia's ridge land were hardy people. Jenna and her family were of that breed. They lived on a rocky ridge farm in the western part of the state, and it was a hard life. They grew what they could in that rocky ground; and what they couldn't grow, they traded for at the general store. Eggs for coffee, butter for sugar or the occasional bag of fine white flour. And what they couldn't grow or trade for, they gathered from the forest around them. The forest provided lots of good food for those wise enough to know what was what. In the springtime, Jenna sent the children out to search for the early mushrooms called "Molly Moochers" in those parts, and morels in other parts of the world. There were wild ramps to liven up the leftover winter potatoes, and greens of all kinds.

One day Jenna's two children, Annie Rose and Jacob, returned from school to find their mother waiting for them on the porch of their cabin home.

"The molly moochers are up, Bob Johnson tells me. Why don't you two git some baskets and go hunt some for our supper? I could surely favor a fine mess of 'em tonight."

The children grabbed two oak-split baskets and hurried excitedly off into the woods. They followed their usual trail down into the hollow behind their house.

The bog oaks and poplars were just beginning to leaf out, and the ferns were uncurling their leaves in the shape that gave them the name "fiddleheads." The air was cool and damp; and as the children traveled down the trail between rocks and roots, the daylight dimmed to a pale green. They didn't notice. They were on a quest, and they could taste the crispy fried mushrooms already.

Although they looked in all their favorite places, they found only a few small mushrooms. Annie Rose looked in her basket, then in her brother's and said, "Why don't we split up? We can search more places that way. Bob ain't that good a mushroom hunter, and if he found 'em, they got to be here somewhere. You take that trail across the hill, and I'll go down towards the creek. We'll meet right back here after the sun goes behind the ridge."

"Okay," Jacob agreed, "Fine with me. Bet I find more than you!" He took off at a quick trot along the path.

Annie Rose walked more slowly down her path. It had been a while since she'd been down this particular trail, and she tried to remember where it went. They usually took the quicker, less steep path from the barn down to the creek. This one was trickier, lots of big boulders and slippery gravel. She wondered if the snakes were still hibernating.

"Be my luck," she thought, "to come up on a slow ol' rattler just wakin' up."

She continued along the trail, looking in the soft decaying leaves under the poplars for the morel mushrooms unmistakable head. She found a few, enough to encourage her to keep looking. After a while she looked up, and frowned.

"I should have been to the creek by now. How did I get here? I disremember them big rocks there."

She stared at the two big sandstone boulders standing on either side of the trail. As she gazed at them, confused and trying to get her bearings, she saw something that made her catch her breath.

An old woman was making her way slowly along the path towards Annie Rose. She was bent with age, and walked with the help of a large crooked stick. She carried a basket on her arm, filled to overflowing with roots and bits of plants. Her white hair stood out like a halo around her wizened face.

Annie Rose stared. "Who was this? How on earth did this old woman get so far down here in the woods?" As she watched the old woman's movements, she realized who this was.

"Oh no! It's that crazy ol' Gracie! Mama told us not to go near here. Her cabin must be nearby. How did I get so close? I thought I was over . . ."

Her thoughts trailed off as she remembered what she had heard about Gracie.

"She's crazy, that one is," her mother had said. "Lives down there in that cabin all alone, always got somethin' cookin' in that big pot of hers. Folks say she spends her days out wanderin' the hills, pickin' and pullin' up who-knows-what, cookin' up them potions of hers.

"Bob says she always knows when's someone's sick, and comes at night and leave brown bottles of that stuff she makes by their doors. Never knocks or nothin', just leaves it there for them to find. Them as is brave enough to take it usually get well, and they leave a little somethin' on the doorstep next night for her—fresh eggs or butter, sometimes money even.

"But no one goes 'round her, because she strange. She ain't like us, Annie Rose. I don't want you children around her, you hear? No tellin' what she might do to you with them herbs and roots of hers. Y'all stay away from her, you hear me? Promise me, Annie Rose." Jenna's dark eyes were troubled and frightened, so Annie Rose promised. Her mother looked a little better after that.

And now here she was, in the woods with that ol' crazy woman, and Annie Rose had no idea where to run because she didn't even know where she was. "A fine howdy-do," she thought to herself in a panic. "Now what do I do?"

The old woman stopped, and stretched a shaking hand toward Annie Rose.

"Child, you're lost, aren't you? Gracie can show you the way out of the woods, not to worry. I can show where to find what you've come for too—if you'll trust me, Child." Her hand stayed stretched toward Annie Rose, and without thinking, the girl moved toward the old woman and took the dry hand in her own.

"How do you know what I've come for?" she asked.

"You're wanting the mushrooms, aren't ye? I can show you where they grow thick on the ground. This way . . . "

They set off and in just a few minutes they were in a sheltered clearing full of the magical morels. Annie Rose picked her basket full. As she reached for one last mushroom, she saw that the sun was gone and dark was falling quickly. She looked at Gracie and said hesitantly, "I surely appreciate your help, ma'am. I need to get back to my brother now."

"Of course you do, child. He's waiting for you just where you told him to. Come, let's go this way. It will take only a few minutes to reach him."

Gracie was right. In a few minutes Annie Rose saw Jacob waiting impatiently on the path ahead. She turned to thank the old woman, but Gracie was nowhere in sight.

"Where did you git all them mushrooms?" Jacob asked in astonishment. "Great Scott! That's a real mess of 'em, that is."

"Never you mind where I got 'em," Annie Rose replied. "We got to git home right now."

They hurried up the path to house, and Annie Rose gave her basket to Jenna.

"My goodness! We'll have a fine supper tonight!" Jenna's pleased face was all the reward Annie Rose needed for her strange afternoon. She did not tell her mother about Gracie. "What good would it do?" she reasoned to herself. "She'd just fret, and there weren't no harm in it. She's just an old lady, that's all, and she likes to live by herself. People ought not talk so about her."

The next day Annie Rose ran home from school. After her chores were done, she ran down the path into the woods, taking the same trail she had the day before.

It wasn't long before she saw a halo of gleaming white hair shining among the spring leaves, and she called out,

"Gracie! Gracie! Here I am. I said I'd come back, didn't I?"

Gracie looked up in surprise, them a gentle smile lit her face. "Hello, Child. So you did return. I was not sure you would. Let me show you what I have in my basket."

The two heads bent over the basket, and slowly they made their way together into the deep woods.

Each day after that, Annie Rose went to visit Gracie. She never told her mother where she was going, but she brought back so many good things in her basket that Jenna did not think to ask. Jacob wanted to go with her, but Annie Rose refused. "Find your own stuff!" she told him. "I don't want you tailin' after me. I got things to do."

One day Jacob was sitting forlornly on the porch of the cabin, and Jenna, seeing him looking so sad, said, "Go play with Annie Rose, Jacob. You needn't sit here alone like that."

"I can't. She won't let me go with her."

"Go with her where? Where does she go every afternoon, anyway?"

"I don't know. She won't tell me and she won't let me go with her either. She said it's none of my business, and not to go cryin' around to you about it either."

"Oh, really!" Jenna looked at him in surprise.

To tell the truth, she'd been so busy herself, she'd paid no mind to the girl's doin's. She always got her chores done, and she always got home in time for supper, usually carrying a basket loaded with wild things to eat. Jenna thought a moment, "How did Annie Rose even know what all that stuff was? Who was showing her?" She felt uneasy, and looked at Jacob with troubled eyes.

"Tell you what, Jacob. Tomorrow when she goes into the woods, you follow her. Be real quiet and sneaky, like a deer. See where she's goin' to. And then come back and tell me. Little Missy might need taken down a peg or two."

"Yes, Ma'am!" Jacob was delighted with this charge. He couldn't wait to follow his mother's orders.

The next day, Annie Rose skipped down the path as she always did, unaware that Jacob was watching and waiting. As soon as she was out of sight, he slid from his hiding place and followed. He had fun trying to walk without making a sound, hiding behind trees and bushes. "I'm just like one of them scouts," he thought proudly. "She won't never see me."

And she didn't. Annie Rose hurried down the trail, thinking about what she would do that day with Gracie. The old woman had promised to show Annie Rose her herb garden this day, and Annie Rose couldn't wait. "There's chamomile to make you hair shine, Child, and lavender to help you sleep. Comfrey for what ails you, roses to make a fine wash for your pretty skin."

The cabin was just ahead, and Annie Rose called out, "Gracie! Gracie! I'm here! Did you think I was never coming?"

Behind her on the path, Jacob sucked in his breath. He watched wide-eyed from behind a witch hazel bush as on old lady with the whitest hair he'd ever seen came out and wrapped Annie Rose in her wrinkled arms.

"Child! It's so good to see you. Just let me take care of this and then we can get to work."

The old woman walked over to the big pot steaming over a wood fire in the middle of the yard. She grabbed the handle of the stirrer and began stirring the dark mixture in the pot. And as she stirred, she sang,

Woodland roots and meadow herbs
Release for me your magic spell

In the kettle I stir and stir
Gracie knows how to make folks well

Jacob watched, transfixed. Gracie! This was ol' crazy Gracie! Mama had told them not to go around here, and here was Annie Rose, comin' down here to her cabin every day!

"Oh boy, wait til Mama hears this! Annie Rose is goin' to git in so much trouble! Mama is goin' to be so mad!" He crept quietly from his hiding place, and then when he was out of hearing, he raced up the trail towards home.

"Mama! Mama! Wait til you hear what Annie Rose been adoin'! Boy, you're gonna have to whup her, Mama. Oh boy, she done it now!" He was so out of breath he had to stop and hold his sides on the porch. His mother came out and stared at him.

"What on earth are you talkin' about, Jacob? Settle down boy, and make some sense."

"I know where she's been a-goin', Mama. Every day, she's been goin' down in the woods to that ol' Crazy Gracie's cabin. That's where she's been. That's how she knows about all that stuff. That's . . . "

"Hush, Jacob, you're makin' my head hurt with your racket. Let me think, will you?" Jenna stood quietly for a moment, her thoughts racing. Then she turned to Jacob and smiled.

"Thank you kindly, Jacob. You been a good boy, you done just what I asked you to do. Now go on inside and eat your supper. I'll speak to your sister when she gets home."

"But, Mama, ain't you gonna whup her? You'd ought to . . . "

"Enough, Jacob! Get inside and leave me to tend to your sister."

"Yes'm," Jacob said glumly. He turned and stepped heavily into the house. He couldn't believe he was going to have to miss Annie Rose gettin' in trouble. She hardly ever did, and he was always into something, that got him on his Mama's wrong side.

It just wasn't fair. He sat down and plunked his elbows on the table, for once not interested in the food before him.

Jenna sat down in her favorite rocker and rocked slowly back and forth, waiting for Annie Rose. When she saw her daughter's bright head approaching, she drew in her breath. The girl looked so happy! What in the world was she doin' with that old crazy woman? What had the old woman been teaching her? Jenna felt a dark helplessness creeping into her heart. If only I wasn't always so busy, so much to do all the time. If only their daddy was still livin' . . . seems like I just can't take care of these younguns alone.

"Hi, Mama," called Annie Rose. "What you doin' settin' out here when it's most dark? Is supper ready? I'm starved! And look here what I brought you."

Her voice trailed off as her mother stared at her without answering.

"I know where you been, Annie Rose, and I fear what you've been doin' and learnin'. I told you to stay away from that old woman. I told you her ways ain't our ways, and folks around here don't go around her—or her place. What were you thinkin', girl? Why did you disobey me like that?"

"You don't understand, Mama, she ain't like folks think. She's nice, and she's teachin' me all kinds of things about the woods and the plants and . . . "

"Exactly, Annie Rose. She's teachin' you that heathen stuff she practices down there in that cabin and I'll not put up with it. You're not to go there again, Annie Rose, do you hear me? From now on you stay right here where I can keep an eye on you. I trusted you, I never thought you'd do something like this. How could you, Annie Rose?"

Annie Rose looked down at the ground.

"You don't understand, Mama. She needs me . . . "

"I need you too, and I need you to stay here and keep away from that old woman. Is that clear?" Jenna's voice was trembling, and tears stood in her eyes.

Annie Rose looked at her, and tears welled up in the girl's eyes.

"All right, Mama. I'll do as you say." She hung her head and walked inside without another word. Jenna sank back in her rocker. Annie Rose was a good girl. Maybe she'd forget all that foolishness in a little while. She'd take her to the Revival next month, that's what the girl needed.

For the next two weeks, all went well. Annie Rose stayed home each evening, working quietly around the house or reading on the porch. She seemed subdued, and her eyes were withdrawn and still. Jenna watched her with concern, yet hopeful that before too long Annie Rose would forget her time in the cabin in the woods and return to her former happy self. It was Fall now, and there was so much to do. She'd make apple butter soon, and Annie Rose always loved doing that.

That was when Jenna got sick, really sick. For three days, she tossed and turned with fever. The children went to the neighbors, frightened at their mother's raving and sweats. The doctor was called, something rarely done because no one had money to pay him. He stayed in Jenna's room for an hour, and when he came out, he looked at Annie Rose and Jacob gravely.

"Your mother is very ill," he said. "The next day or two will tell the tale. She may take a turn for the better, or she may . . . She's young and strong, so I have hope that she can fight this off. You two, come here, and let me show you what you need to do for her."

The children listened in silence, their eyes filled with fear. What would become of them if their mother didn't make it? How could it be possible that she would not get well? Surely the doctor didn't mean what he was saying.

The doctor left, and night fell. Jenna tossed and turned, crying out with the terrible dreams that filled her troubled sleep. Her breath came ragged and thin, and she was soaked in sweat. In one of the many dreams of that long night, she saw an old woman with hair like a halo standing by her bed. The old woman was smiling and holding a brown bottle of murky liquid. She held out a spoonful of the stuff to Jenna, and Jenna swallowed. There the dream ended, and she fell into a deep and dreamless sleep for the remainder of the night.

In the morning, her fever had broken and her eyes seemed clearer. She called out for Annie Rose, and the girl ran to her mother, burying herself in her mother's arms and crying with relief. Jacob stood in the doorway, watching, arms folded sternly, but tears were streaming down his cheeks too. His mother would be all right.

Jenna's recovery was sure but slow. She was weak from the illness and moved slowly around the cabin for the next two weeks. One unusually warm autumn day she sat out on the porch in her favorite rocking chair. The air was sweet on her cheeks, and she smiled as she listened to the chickens clucking and scratching in the fallen leaves. Suddenly she remembered the dream of the old woman, and she called to Annie Rose.

"Annie Rose, come here a minute."

"Yes, Mama, what is it?"

"Do you remember when I was so sick that one night? I dreamed some terrible dreams. One of my dreams wasn't as frightening as the others, and for some reason I just remembered it."

"What was it, Mama?"

"I dreamed that an old lady came into my room. She had beautiful shining white hair, and she gave me some medicine from a brown bottle. Was that a dream, Annie Rose, or was she really there? Was Gracie in my room?"

"It wasn't exactly a dream, Mama. It wasn't Gracie, either. It was me, Mama. I couldn't stand it that you were so ill, and I knew she had medicine that could help you. I went to her cabin and got some. I brought it back and gave it to you. I'm sorry, I know I disobeyed you, but I didn't know what else to do."

Jenna sighed. "Girl, what am I going to do with you? What was in that stuff anyway?"

"I don't know, Mama. She was going to teach me to make it, but then I had to quit going down there."

"Yes, well," Jenna didn't know what to say to that. "What on earth was this? What did that old woman know that even the doctor didn't? Or would she have gotten well anyway, without the brown medicine?"

"That's all, Annie Rose. I don't know what to say to you . . ."

The dogs began barking and running to the gate, and in a moment their neighbor Bob Johnson appeared.

"Howdy, Jenna," he called. "Howdy, Annie Rose. Did y'all hear the news? You know that crazy old woman who lived in that cabin in the woods? Crazy Gracie? Well, I was by there yesterday and there weren't no smoke coming from her chimney, and the fire was out under that big pot of hers. Seemed odd, so I went and looked in the window, just to check on her, you know. And she was layin' in there on the bed. Door was unlocked so I went in . . . and she was dead, Jenna. Just layin' there dead. Looked like she'd been sick for a while, and someone had been comin' and takin' care of her. They must have stopped comin' and she just died."

Bob's voice trailed off and he looked at Jenna in surprise. Jenna had sat straight up and she was looking wildly around the porch.

"What the . . ." Bob started to ask.

"Annie Rose! Anne Rose! Where are you Annie Rose?" Jenna cried. The girl was nowhere to be seen. Bob stared at Jenna.

"You all right, Jenna? Anything I can get you?"

"I've got to find her! I've got to go . . . I know where she is." Jenna stood up, weakness and fear making her legs shake beneath her. She ran from the porch, down through the yard, and found the path to the woods. She ran down that path as if she had traveled it every day of her life. She knew where the path would lead her, and it did. She found herself in a small clearing in the woods, and a small cabin stood in front of her.

The door to the cabin was open and as Jenna stopped to catch her breath she saw her daughter, her beautiful Annie Rose, come out the door and into the yard.

Annie Rose was tying a large apron around her waist, and in her hand was a long, crooked stick. She walked to the pot in the center of the yard, put the stick in and began to stir.

Woodland roots and meadow herbs
Release for me your magic spell
In the kettle I stir and stir
Help me make my Gracie well

"Annie Rose! Annie Rose! Come to me, honey, come to Mama. Gracie is dead, Annie Rose. She's dead, and you can't help her. Come on, honey, come home. Please, Annie Rose," Jenna pleaded.

The girl turned and Jenna saw the beautiful face of her daughter Annie Rose. But the eyes . . . the eyes were the eyes of Gracie. Annie Rose stared at her mother without a word, then turned back to the pot.

Woodlands roots and meadow herbs
Release for me your magic spell . . .

Jenna turned and slowly made her way back up the path. Annie Rose did not watch her mother leave. Annie Rose stirred and stirred and stirred that pot, stopping only when the sun went down to light the fire under the kettle.

Day after day Jenna went back to plead with her daughter, but the girl never seemed to even see her. She went about her work at Gracie's Cabin, and soon Jenna gave up. Her daughter was gone, and her son needed her. She sent food and other supplies down to Annie Rose with Bob Johnson, who dropped them off when he checked his trapline.

"She's doin' all right, Jenna. You needn't worry. I got her a pile of wood for winter, and that garden had plenty of food to last her. She's a smart girl, your Annie Rose. She'll be fine."

One day Bob came back with a different report. "I seen your girl down there in the woods, Jenna. She was walkin' around with a basket on her arm, and had a big stick to walk with. She was talkin' to someone, but there weren't anyone there. But she looked fine, Jenna, and happy. She really is."

And then in the Spring Bob came in and sat down on the porch. "I was down by your daughter's cabin in the woods, Jenna. It was weird. I could hear voices so I went closer. Thought she had company and maybe she was finally comin' out of whatever's been ailin' her. But there wasn't no one there, Jenna. She was talking and laughing inside the cabin. I snuck up and peeked in the window, but I swear there was no one there.

"Then she came outside so I hid real quick. She walked right over to that big pot and began stirring it. And she was singin' the strangest song."

Woodland roots and meadow herbs
Release for me your magic spell
In the kettle I stir and stir
Annie Rose, Annie Rose can make Gracie well.

Mary M. Terry

Key to a Door

It sounded like a dunk—not like a basketball (she hated basketball)—a dunk and a small splash, like a kid into a river from the side of a raft, a short drop into it, so no big sound and no big splash. So she stood and looked: they were lying in the sunken inset at the bottom of the toilet, her keys. Then, hidden by the toilet paper floating like a cloud over them; how the child disappears, too, into the dark, murky water, lost for a second or more, the mother watching from the bank of the river, wondering if she should stand up, walk out and look down into it.

"You gotta be kidding," she thought.

She was standing and pulling her pants up, staring. Funny how the paper floated (it looked like a tent now bent by the wind) when nothing else was moving. Then, from the stall beside her, the swooshing flush of a power toilet sounded strong enough to suck away the keys lying in her toilet with it and maybe her, too. Another toilet flushed and the other women in the restroom were shuffling in and out of other stalls. There had been a line when she had entered the stall. There were lines everywhere in Chapel Hill, lines to do everything. The hand-dryer blew with force and the women chatting raised their voices. Had the other women in line behind her heard the plop of the keys into the water? There were four stalls, but while they waited were they staring at her feet—another reason to hate public restroom: insufficient stall doors—starting to wonder, "Why is she turned around facing the toilet? Is she sick? Why doesn't she just flush and leave?" They would be shifting their weight from one leg to the other.

Maybe she would, just flush and forget about it. *Go on, do something, move*; the voice in her head was Betsy Stapleton's. Bossy Betsy, lumbering toward her on the playground in fifth grade, already smirking. As Betsy approached she would be sitting on the ground; the sun glinted over Betsy's shoulder, until she was over her, peering down, and blocking it.

She, staring, still at the mass of fifth-grade girl above her, had never been athletic, not even active. She liked to read and stay inside, both of which distinguished her not only from most of her classmates but also from her three brothers. They were big and they worked on the farm, put their large bodies to adequate use. She didn't, it seemed, and because she was tall, as the athletic girls were, there was little shelter for her amid the timid and less coordinated shorter girls, with whom she felt most kinship. She stood out like a capital letter mid-word. The taller, stronger and faster girls, like Betsy, singled her out, dared her into foot races. The gym teacher would match her up against one of them—one-on-one dodge ball or relays races—because of their similar size; she always lost.

Why was she tall when everything she wanted she could do short? She never wanted to reach high-up things; sitting was fine with her, in a chair, reading. She never understood her body—its length and size, its movements, where to put it, why it did what it did and not what she wanted. It had never grown in the directions she had wanted. It was a child, unruly, one she did not understand: a mystery. All she wanted, it withheld it from her. And put her instead in situations she hated: tall and she couldn't play sports; long legs and she couldn't run well; even being a woman, it was a tease. She couldn't do what she wanted as one.

As she turned from the toilet, the stall door came only up to her eyes. Again, her height leaving her looming above adequate cover. She looked out and then sunk, quickly, sitting back down onto the seat. Had anyone seen her, thought she was just dancing around in the stall while at least four other women waited? She hoped not. She didn't mean to annoy.

But she was annoyed. She replayed Betsy Stapleton's voice: deep, deeper than most of the boys' in the class, the age when boys sound like girls and girls run like boys.

Should she? Just leave? She didn't want to fish out the keys, stick her hand in the yellow water, catch the toilet paper, have to wipe her hand on the inadequate, thin toilet paper that would ball up and tear rather than dry her hands and keys. If she flushed and the keys clogged the toilet, she would be nearly finished washing her hands by the time the next woman noticed the water rising, if it would, in fact, rise. (The ring of keys would nearly fit down the drain, she noticed, eyeing the circumference.) Better still, flush and don't even wash, just walk quickly out. Do not run; you'll trip, she told herself. Out the door and gone by the time the next occupant noticed, unlocked the stall, and peeked out to look for her: "Are those her *keys*, in the bottom of the toilet there?"

She thought. Her house key: her husband had one. There was another one in a drawer somewhere, maybe two or three. Harris Teeter card: who cares? It never saved her anything she could not get cheaper by driving a few miles more to Food Lion. She should start shopping at Food Lion. She could.

They had started shopping at Harris Teeter when they bought this house, stupid house, bigger than anything two people needed. Her parents had raised four children in a house half the size of this one, and they'd been fine. This one had a ridiculously huge garage that stuck out like a balled-up fist, sticking out more than the house itself. The front door was hidden deep inside a porch-like alcove. The descriptions of the house on the realtor's website called it "a quaint front porch." Hardly. A tiny slit at best, like an opening in a pop-up toaster—dark and narrow. It didn't matter, though, because nothing was coming in or going out it. She and Darryl used the garage door; they didn't have guests.

She never liked Harris Teeter.

The car key: of course that was it, the thing that kept her still sitting instead of leaving without the keys. If she did not reach in for the keys, there she would be: if not locked in the stall, stuck in the library, unable to leave without calling her husband. The people who had attended the program—a reading by a local author—would leave; everyone would leave; the librarian would want to, and she—she stood and stared, sighing at the inevitability of the situation—would not be able to reach her husband. No secretary yet because he was new. Never at his desk because he was still learning things in other areas of the company. He would not answer his cell phone and wouldn't return the call because he never checked the messages until the evening. Why did he even have a cell phone? Lovely unreachable Darryl.

Not that on a good day she cared. A good day, she must have been thinking of Laurel Grove, her hometown in the mountains of North Carolina where she'd lived, except for college, her entire life until a few months ago. She hadn't experienced what she would call a good, whole day since they moved. There were good parts—the reading she'd just attended, for example, was nice, always nice being read to. She had bought the author's book and had already read the first page while waiting in line for the bathroom. It was sticking, bottom up, from her purse, which hung on the stall door.

It was sticking out, like her feet below the door. She looked for a way to pull them up; she had always stuck out. Was there somewhere to rest them, short of squatting on them on the seat of the toilet? Nothing, so they stayed there for anyone who entered to see.

And even though the exposure felt like an everyday occurrence—too short pants that revealed too much of her ankle to be fashionable, too short long-sleeved shirts that rode above her wrists—she was remembering that lately she hadn't been seen. Unlike so much of her experience, sticking out, she had been taken and hidden in their move to Chapel Hill. Hidden below her husband, inside this new house, underneath all the boxes and new things they'd bought and been given for this house, lost in all the unpacking with which her mother-in-law had helped. She couldn't find anything, not a spatula for spaghetti or the water filter.

What she had wanted—the hiding—but she hadn't thought of the fact that hiding sometimes leaves one lost.

She would have to reach in and get them. She imagined pushing her hand into the yellow water. Remember to remove the ring.

On her right hand there was just the one. A gold band with two stones: her husband's birthstone (a sapphire) and hers (a pearl). A gift for their fifth anniversary, just two weeks ago. A mother's ring, she still thought every time she looked at it, because that's what it was to replace. Instead of replacing, as in removing and renaming, it just confirmed for her what she wasn't and that instead of children she had a ring and a husband and the too big house in which he gave it to her. He called it a wife's ring when he handed her the box: "Sometimes less is more," he had said.

She looked at the ring in the open box in her hand. "Fewer," she corrected and looked at him.

He looked at her, his smile now confused by her word. What had she meant? Didn't she like it? The questions hung in his eyes.

"Fewer," she repeated, "fewer stones," she paused, "to represent fewer family members." She was looking at the ring; the sapphire was dark, like the pupil of an eye.

"Right," he understood and looked at the ring and then the carpet, new and already a spot from spaghetti they had eaten in the den the night before; the kitchen table hadn't been delivered yet.

They were both silent.

"But do you like it?" he wanted to move on, drop what they couldn't have and look at what they did. "You like blue."

It meant something to him. He thought she would like it because it was symbolic. She wanted to be a writer, after all. But she couldn't make the stones there tucked in gold represent the two of them. And even if she could've she wasn't sure it would've mattered, would've been what she wanted. The stones were, instead, the pupil of an eye and a little white surrender flag. He was giving up.

"It's nice," she said and hugged him. The air around them smelled like paint, from the new robin's egg blue in the kitchen.

If she did not reach in for the keys, she would be left. Boxed up. Stuck.

If she knew anyone else in Chapel Hill, she would not do it. But since they had just moved there a month ago, she knew no one. Her husband had gotten a job—electrical engineering— in the Research Triangle. While working on his Masters degree in Raleigh, he had done an internship with this company. She had always thought that even though he had moved back to Laurel Grove after he finished his degree (she had finished the previous year, major in English and had returned to Laurel Grove to teach, maybe; she liked kids), she knew that he would eventually get tired of the commute to the plant an hour away from their town. There weren't many other opportunities for him there. He'd moved home to be with her; they'd lived there for nearly five years together. She knew she should be glad to move for him now. But she hadn't been.

Chapel Hill was "quaint," people had told them. Quaint, she thought, like the "porch" on their house. Quaint wasn't something a person from the country looked for anyway. She wanted space and some people, in that order. And with the people, she wanted connection, real community. Chapel Hill met none of those needs. There were certainly people aplenty, but she knew none of them and was convinced that she had nothing in common with them—they were twenty-year-olds, city people. This was a cute community to them. It was a crowded mess to her. She didn't know her way around, through the streets and side-roads and unmarked one-way back alley streets (everyone who lived there knew they were one-way; she did not know, not until the front of her car small Honda was nose-to-nose with an impatient college student's black 4Runner).

She should get out more, though; really get to know people.

This idea came in a different voice, a nasalized one. Maybe it was a character, a start to a story. She looked up, and her blurry reflection in the brushed metallic surface of the stall door was unrecognizable: an indistinguishable mass. Only the white of her shirt was evidently distinct from the rest of the reflection. Her purse covered the space where her face could have shone.

Nope, the nasal voice was, she remembered, the realtor's, Jane Stay. Jane had talked to Darryl and her as they looked at houses like they, all three, had shared years of inside jokes and common concerns. She had tried to like Jane, tried to smile with her at stupid comments about the inferiority of other cities and towns to Chapel Hill; she tried to care about the Tar Heels when Jane mentioned them, frequently. She had felt like throwing up when they finally finished the deal.

"She was nice," her husband had said. "Glad we got someone good. Seemed like she knew what she was talking about." He was looking at the crown molding in the living room, tracing it with his index finger.

"The praises of Chapel Hill," she had thought, but not said, "that's all she 'seemed to know.'" Jane had told her she would

"find people so nice here," in an exaggerated southern drawl.
She had thought Jane was making fun of her accent.

There were people everywhere, young, in-shape (everyone
ran here), energetic, blondes, mostly. That was what she had
seen, and they moved by the hundreds, it seemed. And not just
students. Young parents, too, toting toddlers, pushing them in
big-wheeled strollers through the grocery aisles, at the circula-
tion desk, as they ran along sidewalks and across the streets
while she, stopped, glaring over the steering wheel at them,
was trying to find her way. The road was for driving, after all,
not walking.

And like her in crowded lines at the bank, the houses, too,
all nearly touching, wrapped around, like holes on a belt, the
curve of a small cul de sac. Yards grew into other yards on both
sides, except for those with fences. Fences only for the name—
yours and mine—or maybe a dog every once in a while. That
was their house, in the cul de sac; the one with no "Dead End"
sign stuck at the turn onto their road. Why not? It was. No outlet. She hated Chapel Hill.

She was ready to return to Laurel Grove, return and be
proven right. Return and get out from among the proximity of
people and houses all nearly touching. Tell her mother, "Can you
believe it?" and start with stories of lines of people everywhere,
a wait for everything—the grocery store, lines of traffic—runners running the streets and houses within a stone's throw.

She sighed. Her legs hurt. She had tried to run. Yesterday
after Darryl left for work she looked at her tennis shoes. They
were still white, after two seasons; she had only ever worn them
for aerobics she did inside to VCR tapes. She wanted to try it,
to catch the spring fever that the radio DJs and local television
anchors had been talking about for two days—the warm spell
here in March.

It was like a spell, she thought when she returned after ten
minutes of running, but she had broken through it, was no

longer under it. Her legs were aching and she was gasping. In the third day of the unseasonably warm weather the humidity had moved in. Her lungs couldn't fill fast enough; she felt like she was under water. She remembered why she never ran, not in hot weather, not ever.

Chapel Hill was like a spell, too. (She had hoped it would be a short one, maybe a temporary arrangement for her husband. That seemed unlikely, though; he loved his job.) Everyone there seemed to be under the spell. If you did not love the place, the people, the basketball team, you existed in an alternative universe. You saw the same sights, heard the sounds—especially on basketball game days, blasting from every restaurant and bar— but you could not communicate. The people she saw seemed to be engrossed in all of it, and she was unable to break through to them. She felt like she was knocking; no answer.

Maybe she was not knocking.

She looked through the crack between the stall door and the wall. No one. The noises around her had completely stopped. One woman came in, entered a stall, two doors away. She sat silently for a second, not moving, until she heard the woman flush. She exhaled. The woman came out of the stall, washed and left. She doubted the woman had even seen her feet. Fly on a wall, or in a wall, she thought.

Maybe she was retreating. Waiting for life here to pass over, like a storm—noisy, unknown, something that kept her inside. She thought about staying inside, inside the new house, which she did not like; inside her car, away from the lines of people and the runners; inside this stall even. Marriage had been her first successful attempt at retreating, a hiding beside someone taller than her—her brothers and parents never were that for her; they did other things. But Darryl was like her; he read and liked to stay home. They would sit together and when they sat, stand together when they stood; she wouldn't be the tallest. Wouldn't be the one everyone saw first. She'd take it.

But sitting in the stall, the insufficient stall that revealed her below and, if she stood, above, she recognized the futility of hiding. What would it take to break her out? Would something, instead, break in? In the novel from which the author, a professor at the university, had read there had been a break-in, a fatal one. In a mess of broken glass, rumpled rug and a ringing telephone the young protagonist had found her neighbor murdered.

Violence always came to mind when she considered breaking out, changing things. The move to Chapel Hill hadn't been violent but, instead, a steady, slow move, because, it had moved her further in, hidden her. But she wanted out. Out of the new house, out of Chapel Hill, out of her body. Out of her marriage? She didn't know. Nothing was distinct. The impulses were a muddled mess. She didn't know which out was the answer. She had to know if something lived inside by now; they had been married five years. It had to come out. It would be violent and bloody, like surgery, a delivery. Good violence, though — there was good violence that led to life. She raised her chin from resting it on her bent arm. Her arm: pale skin, pale from winter and long-sleeves, from staying inside. She felt like a porcelain doll, too fragile to touch, breakable. To be kept locked in a case or high on a shelf.

Just go out: through skin and stall and wall and water.

She stood up, looked down into the toilet — paper still swimming, hiding then reveling the keys; it was a matador. She was ready. At least there was only water and piss to go through.

The door to the restroom opened. The air in the room changed, cooler, and she heard voices from the library. She turned her head toward the stall door. Feet were approaching sliding across the floor. They stopped at her stall door. She stood silently, wondering how long she had been in there.

A knock. "Ma'am, are you ok?" the woman's voice sounded like her own, a distinct twang.

"Hmm?" she tried to sound surprised. She paused. "Yes, thank you."

Silence.

"Do you need any help?"

"No, no. Thank you, though," she thought how absurd she must sound. Who was this woman who sounded like she could be from Laurel Grove asking her questions? She paused. "I dropped my keys."

"Are they in the toilet?" the woman asked.

"Yes," she was watching them, arching herself over the toilet now, like they were held by her gaze and might escape if she moved.

"Oh," the woman sounded relieved and then jovial; "Wait one second," and the bathroom door swung open again over the floor with a sweeping sound.

She waited behind the stall door. Should she go out? This woman would return; she did not want the woman to reappear when she was stepping out of the stall. She did not want the woman to think she was asking her to sift through the mess to retrieve the keys. She would stay in the stall.

The restroom door opened again.

"You're gonna love this thing." As the woman spoke, she could hear a clicking; the woman was working on something. "I reckon we've all been there before."

There was a pause and a few more clicks. "Here." The woman shoved an object that looked like a silver pointer under the stall door; "this works like a charm. Just stick it in the bowl and fish them out. It's magnetic, so it'll bring them up for you."

She took the silver wand. She listened as she looked over the toilet. The woman must work at the library. She was standing probably facing the stall door between them, as if she were watching the process. The scene from above, they were in a row: the librarian immediately behind the skinny stall door (nearly imperceptible from above, just an inch-thick line drawn between them), and her waving the wand over the toilet. She knew the librarian would be standing closer to her than if the door were not there. The woman was probably breathing on its metallic face, a fog forming.

She was holding the thick end of the wand. She slid the other into the water. The floating paper wrapped around the wand. She pulled it up, the wad of paper dripping. It sounded like interference on an intercom.

"Did you get them?" the librarian asked from the other side of the door.

"No, not yet," she felt like a surgeon. The librarian behind her was the nurse, passing the instrument, waiting for updates or further instructions. "That was the paper. It wrapped around the tip."

"Oh," the woman paused. "Do you need some help?"

"No, I think I can get it now, nothing obscuring my view." She put the wet paper on the seat.

She had planned on inserting the tip of the wand through the key ring, but the second she touched the tip to the metal key ring, it stuck. She pulled them up and out, leaning back nearly into the stall door. She did not want the splashes of urine and water to hit her pants.

Again the dripping, louder this time.

"Did you get them?" the librarian asked.

"Yes." She covered her palm with dry toilet paper and grasped the keys. Then she threw the wet wad from the seat back into the toilet and flushed.

She turned to face the stall door. She could see just over the stall door to the top of the librarian's head, dark hair. The woman was short. She took her purse from the hook and pulled the door open.

The librarian backed up, and she held the keys up between their faces and smiled. This had to be her oddest encounter ever with another person.

The librarian smiled. "Good for you!" she said. "That thing works wonders. Everyone should have one."

"Yeah, I guess so," she said and handed the wand to the woman. She washed her hands and the keys. She reached for more soap.

She turned off the water and shook her hands. The librarian reached in front of her and grabbed a paper towel and handed it to her; then the librarian took the keys from her hand and dried them.

"Thank you," she said. She held out her hand, "I'm Sarah."

"I'm Carol Ann; nice to meet you," the librarian said, shaking Sarah's hand.

"Well, here you go," Carol Ann held out the keys toward her.

"Thank you," Sarah looked at the keys. The house key, the newest one, a silver Kwikset with three little windows along its arched top, was shining, reflecting the iridescent lights of the restroom. "You've been very helpful."

Carol Ann smiled. She was younger than Sarah, by a few years, maybe twenty-nine. Her small nose turned up at the end; a friendly nose, Sarah thought.

"It's happened to me before, but it was before I worked here and I didn't have one of these things." Carol Ann held up the silver wand that now looked more like a pen because she had shortened it by pushing it back down into itself. "So I had to reach in and get them." They walked out of the restroom, and Carol Ann looked around the library as she spoke.

"Have you worked here long?" Sarah asked.

"I guess," Carol Ann paused and thought, looking up, "nearly five years, since I moved from Toursville."

"Toursville? In the mountains?" Sarah's voice sounded more surprised than she wished it had.

"Yeah. You heard of it?" Carol Ann asked in an even tone.

"I'm from Laurel Grove," she had stopped walking and was looking at Carol Ann. "We just moved. A month ago," she was considering how much to say.

"Well, welcome to Chapel Hill," Carol Ann said and smiled. Her eyes nearly closed when she did.

"Thank you." It was all she needed to say, even though she could have said much more but every sentence would have started with thank you—for having brown hair, for being from the mountains, for working here, for the wand. Sarah looked down instead, one second, and then back up; it was the period to her unsaid thank-you's. "Did you come here to go to the University?"

"Yeah, and got this job right out of school."

Sarah smiled. "Well, I'm sure I'll see you again."

"Were you here for the reading?"

"Yes."

Carol Ann held up an index finger, turned and walked through a doorway. She was like a child, nearly, not stopping to explain things before she rushed away to bring back something to show Sarah. In the restroom she had disappeared and returned with the wand. Now she was shuffling back to Sarah, extended hand holding a bright blue brochure.

"There's another one next month," she pointed to the white words.

Sarah read.

"Take it with you. If you come, I'll see you then," said Carol Ann, and she turned and walked back through the doorway, out of sight.

The reading would feature a poet from Greensboro, Fred Chappell. A name like a place, like this place.

Not until right then had she thought about the name of a small place—a chapel—inside the name of this town, Chapel Hill.

She walked out the door. A car pulled in beside hers. She watched a woman get out of the driver-side door and open the back doors for two children, a boy and a girl. They were tall as the woman's waist, both brunette. Sarah watched them as she walked toward them. They held hands, one on each side of the woman. They were twins. The woman looked at Sarah as they approached, "Hello," she said.

Sarah turned, surprised at the greeting. "Hello," she said.

They had reached the covered walkway a few meters from the door. The boy and girl had dropped hands and started running, racing to the door. The girl caught it first, opened it, and the boy stopped, dropped his shoulders and walked in. The woman followed.

Sarah opened her car door. She threw in her purse and then looked as she stood beside the car, the door like an arm around her. There was a fruit stand across the street. She watched a woman pick up and then press some plums. Sarah could see them clearly. They were still too red, she thought. It was not spring yet.

She sat down. She had been sitting all afternoon. The pamphlet from the library was sticking out of her purse, beside the new book she'd bought. She would go to the next reading and see Carol Ann. Maybe more than getting out, this move to this place could be about not hiding and instead finding, finding who she would be in it; what she brought inside her and how she could grow it there. Maybe soon she would find a seat there, just to listen at first, in her own place, her own small chapel.

Tricia Scott

The Day the Devil Beat His Wife

It is three o'clock in the afternoon, and Ginny has yet to brush her hair or her teeth. She stands, as she does much of the time now, at the bedroom window and watches the road for a sign of his car. She searches for a glimpse of red between the trees. It won't be long now before all the leaves are off, and she won't have to squint so hard. She wouldn't have to squint at all if she could only remember to put her contacts in. Today hundreds of oak leaves spiral and twist past her, drawn off the ground by the wind. They remind Ginny of couples caught up in some wild square dance, twirling from one partner and then to another. She singles out a leaf and tries to follow its path, her eyes managing to track the leaf as the current carries it down the long gravel driveway and out into the road. She sees the leaf spinning high one last time before finally disappearing from sight.

"Good riddance," Ginny says suddenly as she pictures her husband, Carter, as the oak leaf, swept up and blown all the way to another state by Sissy, her best friend since the second grade. A friend who, if Ginny really lets herself think about it, has never been full of much other than hot air anyway.

A clap of thunder rolls down between the mountains and shakes the house, but Ginny doesn't move. The trees bend and sway looking like they could break at any minute, and the wind catches at the gate, sends it whipping back and forth. Soon there will be frost on the windows, and he will still be gone. Deep down inside Ginny knows this and goes to bite her nails, but realizes they're already down to the quick.

This past week has been the hardest since Carter got into the car with Sissy on a Sunday morning almost two months ago. Monday brought with it a toilet that leaked water all around its edges and onto the hardwood floors; Tuesday was the day a step leading up to the porch had fallen off and the furnace had quit working; and on Wednesday she dropped a mirror and it had broken into pieces. Seven years of bad luck, Ginny's father would have told her. On Thursday she heard, "Yesiree, a new furnace is lookin' to cost you in the ballpark of thirty-eight hundred bucks" from a man who looked suspiciously like that comedian Carter loved to imitate so much, Larry the Cable Guy. Carter was always hollering "Git-R-Done" right along with him.

And then to top it all off, last night she had dreamt for the first time in weeks. In her dream one of the branches on the huge oaks surrounding the house had broken off, falling right through the roof and into the bedroom, pinning her to the sheets as she laid wide-eyed and numb and so cold she was turning blue. Sissy was there laughing hysterically and clapping, and Carter was standing over her with a microphone preaching something about the hammer of God. Ginny could tell he was placing the blame on her for all that had gone wrong.

"It's amazing the things a person can get used to," Ginny thinks as she moves from the window and closes the blinds. She overheard a woman say this at the grocery store recently, and she would have to agree. If given enough time, a person could get used to anything.

Ginny eases herself down onto the bed beside her daughter. Sophie is napping, curled into a ball and sucking the thumb on her right hand, holding the edge of the quilt in her left. Ginny feels proud of the quilt. She made it herself four years ago, right after Sophie was born. She had taken scissors to her maternity clothes, had cut the dainty floral patterns into shapes and stitched them together into a crazy quilt. She'd added embroidery and beads, working at night in between nursings and diaper changings. It is a part of herself she plans on giving to Sophie, perhaps on a day years from now when she first hears the news that her daughter is expecting a little one of her own.

Ginny lies back, releases the lungful of air she's been holding tight, and closes her eyes. She can still see her daughter as she was that morning, asking, "Mama, where's Daddy? When's Daddy coming home? Does Daddy love me?" For weeks, Sophie has been asking the same questions, over and over like a stuck record, her tiny perfect hands fluttering around her face like little birds as she talks.

Rain is coming down in sheets, and the sounds of the storm are deafening.

"Can the storm come inside, Mama?" Sophie sits up suddenly and asks, her blue eyes round like silver dollars. Carter used to complain and say that Ginny had turned Sophie into a nervous child.

"No, honey, it'll be all right. I promise. Everything will be all right." Ginny rubs Sophie's back.

"Tell me a story, Mama, a happy one," Sophie begs.

"But I don't have a story, honey," Ginny says and instead sings softly into her daughter's ear. "*Hush little baby, don't say a word. Mama's going to buy you a mockingbird . . .*" This quiets Sophie and they listen to the rain beating a tattoo on the tin roof until Sophie falls again into sleep, heavy and completely, her thumb-sucking once more rhythmic and slow.

Ginny hates it, too, when Sophie worries about things. She's afraid she has shaped her daughter into a miniature version of herself. What if, like the passing of a quilt or some other family heirloom, she has presented her with a life of uncertainty and doubt?

She remembers how Carter certainly never missed a chance to call her a "worry-wart." He would laugh and say, "Virginia

Elizabeth Shively, you are wound entirely too tight. You're about as tight as an eight-day clock." Or "You're as bad as a dog worrying at a bone." Ginny would paste a smile on her face and say, "I resemble that remark" even though she didn't think she was all that bad. She'd say anything not to show how much it hurt and anything to keep down a fuss. Carter was forever after her to relax; he wanted her to change and become a female version of how he saw himself, laid back and calm about everything. She tried, but could never make it work for long. Sometimes she thinks he was just pointing out her imperfections so she wouldn't have time to notice his.

"Why does Daddy love himself so much?" Sophie even asked once, and Ginny had laughed harder at that than she'd ever laughed at anything before in all her life.

Last night, Carter's mother, Francine, stopped by like she did most Fridays these days. It's like she's trying to make up for her son being gone. That's what Ginny thinks, but she tries to be nice because she knows Francine means well. Plus, it's one night she doesn't have to worry herself with cooking. Francine makes wonderful meals, and she always brings Sophie's favorite-homemade three-cheese lasagna and Ginny's favorite-red velvet cake. Ginny bakes the cornbread and makes a salad. After all, she tells herself, it's not Francine's fault her son turned out the way he did.

"You're looking down-right peaked," Francine accused after dinner, while Sophie was in the bathroom. "Have you been taking your vitamins?"

"When I remember," Ginny answered, moving to gaze at her puffy eyes and blotched skin in the dining room mirror. She tried to make a joke, covering up with clichés the way she always did. "I look like I've been rode hard and put up wet."

Francine looked at her but didn't crack a smile.

Carter used to say, "When it comes to beauty, Mama doesn't fool around." Francine had sold Mary Kay for twenty years at least and had the pink Cadillac for ten.

"Ginny dear, I don't want you to take this the wrong way, but we can do a complete makeover on you whenever you feel ready." Her voice was softer now. "You're a beautiful girl. You're not going to get rundown are you? There's Sophie to think of and, remember, there's a whole lot more men out there besides Carter. More fish in the sea. When my Millard died, bless his heart, I just holed up in the house for years. I wasn't a bit of good to anybody."

"And well . . . " she went on before Ginny could reply, "I might as well go ahead and say what I really need to say. I've been dreading it all day." Francine stood up and gathered the dirty plates, the napkins and the forks. She wouldn't look at Ginny. "My sorry excuse for a son called last night."

"Carter called? How is he?" Ginny heard her choked voice and it sounded strange and ugly to her ears. She reached out a hand and placed it on Francine's arm.

"He's still in Asheville and still with that ole hussy and . . . I'm so sorry, Ginny, but he's not coming back. Sissy's three months along."

"Along?" Ginny couldn't understand, not at first.

"Sissy's pregnant."

Ginny felt as if the words themselves had come across the table and slapped her on the face; and she had sat at the table for hours, stunned, unable to speak. Francine didn't try to get her to talk. She gathered Sophie up, played with her in her room, and did the entire bedtime routine before she left quietly, never coming back into the dining room. Ginny was grateful for it.

Twenty-five years. That's how long Ginny has known Sissy. "She's trouble. Mark my words," Ginny's mother would say about her. "She uses you and you let her." Ginny had always defended Sissy, knowing that no matter what she could count on her friend. "Best friends til the end," they would chant in school. She had meant it and she wonders now if this is why it hurts more to think about Sissy's betrayal than it does Carter's.

When Sissy's husband Greg died last year, Ginny had let Sissy come live with them. Sissy had been a mess, carrying on about seeing Greg's ghost everywhere she looked. Ginny had stayed up at night, sitting with Sissy, like a child, until Sophie had gotten the flu and needed her more. Then she'd asked Carter to sit up with Sissy and she guessed that's when it all began. She's figured out that Carter has always had a thing for needy women, and it comforts Ginny some to think that Sissy simply wasn't in her right mind. She can see how already her own mind is trying to change them both around and make them into better people than they turned out to be.

* * * * *

Ginny thinks about all those years she would awake in the mornings, long before Carter, and just lie and watch him as he slept; loving the game of trying to make the rise and fall of her own breath match his. His dark hair was stark against the pale green pillowcase that last morning together. He'd been smiling in his sleep, and she imagined he was dreaming of her. She remembers pushing the hair back from his forehead to better study his face, loving the lines of his eyebrows and the shape of his chin and his jaw line that were the same as Sophie's. That was the morning the light had fallen in patches across the quilt after days of rain. That was the morning she had thought they could all go on a picnic or putt-putting, do something as a family. That was the morning Carter had looked right through her with his great liquid black eyes, eyes like a blackbird's eyes, and told her he was bored with his life and needed a change, needed to "find his truth." He said he stopped loving her years ago, that she brought him down, and he was tired of pretending for Sophie's sake. He'd been sleeping with Sissy for over a month and they were in love. "Deeply in love." All invisible words that seemed to Ginny to be plucked straight out of the air, that's how real they felt.

How could they do this to me?

Her hands clutch at Sophie's quilt, gripping so hard her knuckles turn white and she can feel the agony and rage burning and rising up from her chest, wanting to choke her. She almost wishes it would because her mind is frozen on a single image: Sissy with her wild, red hair and her sleek red nails. The same Sissy, who was maid-of-honor at her wedding, the Sissy who was supposed to be "friends til the end" was waking up every morning beside her husband. Carefree Sissy who never worried, and whom Ginny has never seen look "down-right peaked" a day in her life.

"I hope it's storming in Asheville and they both get struck by lightning," Ginny whispers, rising stiff and shaking from the bed. She wishes that she could grab Sophie up and run with her out into the storm and keep on running and running until she got them to sunshine, and until she got them to happiness.

Sophie's cats, Wynken, Blynken, and Nod are waiting anxiously, and they come rushing to Ginny, tumbling over each other in their eagerness to be fed. She finds she is grateful for mundane, familiar tasks like this one. Even the act of making a cup of hot tea soothes her and stills her shaking hands, from the lonesome whistle of the kettle to the familiar scent that comes from the box of Earl Grey.

Ginny finishes the first cup, drinking while the liquid is still scalding. She eats all but two slices of the left-over cake and finishes two more cups of tea before she notices how the quality of light in the room has changed. The kitchen is so bright she has to shade her eyes. Sunlight is streaming in through the windows over the sink, and yet it is continuing to rain. She can hear it. It is a good, solid steady rain.

Another saying of her daddy's come into her mind. "Sunshine and rain. The devil is beating his wife," she whispers and laughs.

Ginny props the front door open so she can hear Sophie if she wakes up again and needs her. She settles into the porch swing, her bare feet tucked under her body. October sunshine is warm on her face. The memory of another sun shower is wrapping itself around her like a blanket. In her mind, she sees herself as an eleven year old child, a big imagination, long legs and a face full of freckles. She sees her father as he was years before the lung cancer came and ate him up. *Ginny closes her eyes . . . leans slowly back into the cushions . . . and lets the images come . . .*

* * * * *

Ginny moves through the rain and the sun, trying to match her long strides with her father's even longer ones. In their hands are covered buckets of feed for the goats down at the far end of the field. They make it to the fence and the shelter of the pines before they both stop, catching their breath and resting their buckets on the rail. The fence is twined through with blue morning glories and honeysuckle, and Ginny's father has moved closer and has his hand resting on her shoulder. They stand there for what seems to Ginny like hours, each breath drawing in the scent of wet earth and flowers. She watches the sunlight illuminating the raindrops; and the world seems suddenly filled with magic; everything looks lit up from the inside, like she can see the soul of every leaf, every petal.

Her father turns to her and smiles wide. This starts a fluttering in the pit of Ginny's stomach and a tightening in her throat. Yes, this day is magic, she thinks. Maybe this is the day that Daddy is going to start being happy again. She tries but can't recall a single time she's seen a smile since he was laid off work seven months before.

"Devil's beating his wife," he says.

"What in the world are you talking about, Daddy?" Her voice is full of surprise.

He stares down into his hands for a few moments before he turns his attention back to Ginny, "It's what I've always heard.

My daddy always said, 'When the sun's out and it's raining the Devil's beating his wife.'"

"That's just some old saying." Ginny says. She had been hoping for one of daddy's good stories.

Her father shrugs. "Maybe so, but there might just be something to it."

"That's silly, I mean, why would anyone want to marry the Devil? What's she like? Are the raindrops her tears? Why's he beating her? What did she do?" Once the questions started they came tumbling out.

Ginny's father shrugs his shoulders again. "You're the one with the wild imagination. You tell me. I don't guess I ever put much thought to it, to tell you the truth."

"Oh." Ginny is disappointed. Her daddy used to tell such clever stories. He used to tell some about ghosts that left her and Sissy shaking and awake for hours.

"I do seem to recall how Granddaddy Earlie's version had a little more to it. Something like, 'The Devil's behind the kitchen door beating his wife with a frying pan,' her daddy says, rummaging in his pockets for a cigarette.

"I don't get it. Do you, Daddy?" She watches her father light the cigarette with a match.

"I think I saw the Devil once when I was hunting up on the ridge." Ginny's father looks back at her and draws in sharply on his cigarette.

"Are you pullin' my leg?" Ginny giggles. She has forgotten how much he used to like picking on her and her brother, Winston, eight years old yesterday.

Her father doesn't answer but he smiles again, grey eyes shining. He is quiet for a while, staring off at the mountain until finally his face grows serious again.

"I don't believe in the Devil or in God either one sometimes."

Ginny doesn't know what to say. She knows her mother would be angry to hear her daddy talk like that.

When her father speaks again his voice has lost all playfulness. "I'll finish up. You go on in and get dry." He takes the bucket from her hands and without another word walks the rest of the way down the hill. Ginny watches until he disappears behind the barn.

That her father's cheerful mood was gone combined with the thought of the Devil's wife crying saddens Ginny more than she could ever put words to. She puts both hands out to catch as many rain drops as she can, then she brings them up to her face, spreading the wetness over her cheeks. She pretends they are her tears.

Ginny stands there for a while longer until real tears start to fall and blend with the rain, then she walks back up the hill and goes inside the trailer.

"Every good gift and every perfect gift is from above," her mother quotes from the Bible, the book of James, when Ginny tries to tell her about the beauty of the sun and the rain. Her mother knows about as much scripture as Preacher Ingram; and the Devil is as real to her as a neighbor down the road; but she won't listen when Ginny mentions the old saying. "Pure foolishness. You know better than to pay attention to that kind of talk." Ginny's mother looks at her with a smile that never quite reaches her eyes.

The entire time she's helping her mother get dinner ready and on up into the night when she can't sleep, Ginny thinks about the Devil's wife. "Sadness makes us kin," she whispers to the darkened room. It doesn't matter that she knows the wife is made up. She doesn't even know if she believes in the Devil either, but what she does know is what it's like to get a whipping. She knows the feel of a willow switch or a belt across the back of her legs, and she knows the whelps and bruises they can leave.

Ginny gives the Devil's wife a name.

Victoria Rose.

Lying in bed, hands behind her head, Ginny listens to her mother's quiet crying. Her mother is at the kitchen table with her head in hands. A Bible is open on the table in front of her. Ginny wants to go and put her arms around her mother's neck but doesn't, afraid her mother would be angry or embarrassed. She can hear faint snoring from her brother, but she wonders if her father is awake and listening too.

Ginny stares at the ceiling and wills her thoughts to form story. A story of how the Devil and Victoria Rose are brought together and of how the old saying came to be in the first place.

Ginny pictures the Devil as a shape emerging from a hole in the trunk of a large oak, just like the one outside her window. The Devil sheds his scarred, old face and layers of rags like the skin of a snake until he is a handsome young man with blond hair and bright green eyes. He wears a white shirt, buttoned to the neck with overalls that are new and creased; his boots are shiny and black. A wife to keep me company, that's what I need, he thinks. He stands deep in the woods, his head tilted back, listening for sounds of music, laughter, something other than the voice of the mountains. Nothing. He walks to a nearby poplar tree and disappears into a hole midway up the trunk. The Devil travels this way through the tree holes, entering one only to emerge in an eye's blink, miles away in another. This is his magic. From sugar maple to hemlock, from chestnut to walnut, he searches the mountains and hollows in search of a woman to take for his wife. On this cold autumn night he leaves the trunk of a pine and wanders deep into the hollow below Poor Mountain. It is here the Devil first hears the faint sounds of a dulcimer and a woman singing. Captivated, he follows the music to a small log cabin set amidst a circle of willow trees.

The woman's voice is low and husky.

"They came upon a cherry tree,
Hung over a bank of mud

And filled to the top with the ripest fruit
As red as any blood."

The owls, whippoorwills, and other night-birds have ceased
their calling; the entire hollow is still and hushed as if straining
to listen. The Devil stands in the dark outside the uncurtained
window, spellbound by the vision he sees within.

Victoria Rose is sitting in a pool of light made by a fire burning hot and bright in the hearth. She is barefoot and wearing a
long white cotton gown which she's pulled up around her knees.
Her wavy dark hair spills down in a tangle around her shoulders
and her body moves slowly to the music. With long graceful fingers, she strums at the strings of the dulcimer resting flat across
her lap.

"The branches knelt before the girl
To let her have her taste;
They rustled to her weary feet
And curved about her waist."

The Devil watches as the firelight plays across her skin like
a live thing, watches as her golden eyes dance with emotion,
her foot tapping a slow easy rhythm on the wooden planks.
Never has he seen a woman as beautiful or heard music so lovely
and pure.

He watches until the first hint of dawn, until her eyes catch
his just beyond the window.

"Good morning to you, sir," is all she has time to say before
he weaves a spell of his own around her, leaps through the window and snatches her up into his arms. He carries her to the
hole in the trunk of a willow where the blackest part of the
night has already gone on before them.

Ginny imagines how the Devil takes Victoria Rose to his
home on the peak of the highest mountain. He continues with

132

his charade, making her happy, making her believe he is an honest man, a good man and Victoria Rose never senses anything false. Soon they are wed. She calls him "her tree spirit" and thinks of him as guardian of all the woods. The Devil finds he is fond of being thought of in this way and takes her on many travels through the tree holes, visiting beautiful places all over the world. Osage orange to round-leaved teak, hawthorn to scarlet oak, cedar to silver birch.

And then, after months, or perhaps it is years of happiness, things begin to change. Gradually, like the closing of a beautiful flower or the turning of an autumn leaf, the Devil grows tired of being good and reveals his belligerent and ugly self to Victoria Rose. "I am not the spirit of the trees," he says to her one cold night, "I am the thing that rots the limbs and breaks the boughs. The leaves shake with fear, they tremble when I pass, they cry vainly to the wind for help."

The Devil's spell is broken. Victoria Rose sees his true self and she falls into a sadness deeper than the mountain is tall. He locks her away and forces her to play her dulcimer and sing for hours at a time. The Devil cares only for himself and doesn't seem to notice if her fingers bleed or her throat aches from singing songs of happiness.

Many weeks pass. Victoria Rose discovers that by closing her eyes as she is singing and playing it is possible to imagine herself back in her cabin. She forgets her pain, losing herself in the music, and soon discovers the Devil does as well. If she plays slow ballads, he will fall asleep, sometimes sleeping for days. If it is a fast and lively tune, he will dance until finally collapsing in a heap at her feet, once not waking for an entire month.

"My life is what I make it," Victoria Rose begins to say to herself at the start of each new day.

When "Old Scratch," as she now secretly calls him, requests she play a ballad, she strums the softest, slowest tune she can recall and there are times, though rare, when he falls asleep before forgetting to lock the door, leaving her to travel alone through the tree holes. Victoria Rose walks in the warmth and stretches out lazy and long in the cool beneath her willow trees. She wanders through the honeysuckle and the thickets of wild roses that grow near her cabin, breathing in their sweet perfume. The Devil always awakes and finds her no matter how well she hides herself, wounding her deeply by breaking off a switch from her beloved willows. This is what the Devil uses to beat his wife, not stopping until her tears fall like rain down from the mountain, magical tears that bless those who still remember her.

Ginny imagines she can smell the honeysuckle and wild roses. She wants so badly to go and wake Winston and tell him the story but she doesn't. She can almost hear Victoria Rose's music floating down to her like milkweed on the wind; and she finds herself wondering why her mother, who is still in the kitchen, doesn't come into her room to see about the noise. Ginny plays the story over and over in her mind. She does this on into the night until she hears her mother go back to bed, and until sleep finally comes and swallows her up.

* * * * *

The rain has stopped and the air has grown heavy and still. Sounds start to dance in, the crunch of tires somewhere down the gravel road, the barks of a neighbor's dog, the clock inside striking the hour. Ginny's first thoughts are of Sophie. She is anxious for her to be awake. Ginny hopes her daughter will ask her again for a story because this time she has one. "Life is what you make it." Ginny says to the trees, glorious old sentinels that have made it through another storm and to the crickets chirping out in the grass. She likes the feeling she gets when she talks out loud and there is no one there to make fun of her and she sits up straighter, brushing her hair back from her face with her hands. She sends up a silent thanks for the memory of Victoria Rose.

"My life is what I make it, damn it," she yells this time, not giving a hoot who hears, not caring if she wakes Sophie. There is nothing she wants more right now than to curl up on the swing with her daughter in her arms. All this time she had been thinking there was less to believe in when maybe there was more.

"Good riddance, Carter," Ginny says, surprised to find that this time she really means it and for this moment at least the sense of having lost something is gone.

"Good-bye, Sissy." These words are harder but they come and they feel good.

Ginny pulls her knees up snug against her chest and breathes in deep. The air smells of recent rain and sunshine and hope.

Tammy Wilson

She Married a Bonehead

For years the women of the Busy Bees Quilters' Guild had heard about Cleo Hudson's blundering, neatnik husband; but that particular day, she appeared distraught and serious.

"I'm leaving Hap," Cleo said.

"Leaving Hap? Surely you'll patch things up," Bernice said in a grandmotherly tone.

"Some things can't be patched," Marjorie said. A divorcee, she knew the bitter regret of rash decisions.

The Hudsons were a study in opposites when it came to tidiness, but any long-term relationship tends to develop a centrifugal motion, feeding upon itself out of mindless habit. Hap and Cleo were no exception. He insisted their home be tidy from the inside out. She, meanwhile, was always a step behind, searching the trash for useable items he'd thrown out: half-used rolls of batting, scraps of fabric, odd knick knacks in the back of a closet.

"I'm a quilter," Cleo said. "I make treasures out of trash," as her friends were well-aware. In the twelve years they'd worked together, Cleo had furnished most of the raw materials and the entertainment.

"No use wasting something that's still good when it could bring cash at a yard sale," she told the group. But during the last one she'd held, when their youngest daughter left home, the couple had nearly come to blows when Hap started to throw away the "merchandise." He was too embarrassed to sell his old things to strangers and allow them to tote off their purchases in Ingle's grocery bags from where he worked.

"He told me, 'They'll think I stole the bags from the store,'" Cleo said.

As she explained, "A neat house is the sign of a dull mind."

She was anything but dull. Without Cleo, the half-dozen quilters wouldn't have had free fabric to stitch, nor would their group have been so tightly knit. Some said that Cleo's misadventures were the thread that held the group together. While the rest of the women stitched several yards, she would barely finish a foot or two, though she proudly wore her patchwork pin which read, I'd Rather Be Quilting.

Cleo's mismatched marriage continued in its own path like the eclectic group who stitched every Tuesday at the Emmanuel Church of God. Earlier that spring, they began a Double Wedding Ring quilt for the Harvest Festival as in-kind payment for use of the church basement. Rain or shine, the women gathered to pool their talents. Last year's project, a red-work embroidered quilt with toile backing was Cleo's brainchild, though a few of the members balked at the extra work required to prepare the top.

"That's twice the trouble of patchwork," Marjorie said, her thick reading glasses perched low on her nose. "I can barely see what I'm doing as it is."

"If you can barely see and you stitch that well, what could you do with twenty-twenty vision?" Eva rubbed her hands. At seventy-two, she had long suffered from arthritis, but said quilting kept her hands nimble. "I hear that Lasik surgery is something."

"It's something all right," Marjorie said. "I know someone who had it done last winter and it cost a thousand dollars out of pocket."

Eva eyed Georgeann. "I sure don't have that much in my pocket."

"Me neither," Shirleen said. A long-time widow, she pinched pennies as second nature.

"Come on, girls, red toile is *in* these days. It'll be our best quilt yet," Cleo said. As usual, the group followed along. The project raised nine hundred dollars, which helped the Emmanuel Aid Society rebuild a home for a burned-out family. The quilters were pleased that their stitchery had helped folks in such dire circumstances.

"Bad luck could be ours some day," said Bernice. She had outlived three husbands and knew all that could go wrong in a marriage, but even her life stories couldn't top Cleo's.

While all of the Busy Bees were on the faded side of middle age, Cleo was among the youngest, even younger than Georgeann, a petite blonde, who was a state debutante until she moved to Country Club Lane as a banker's wife in 1961. He was now retired and she, like some of the other women, used her Tuesday mornings to escape from the role of Woodrow Farthing's wife. The platinum rinse on her hair couldn't fool anyone. Too many Hilton Head vacations had leathered her skin.

Most of the quilters would've agreed that Hap Hudson was a nice fellow, even handsome as middle-aged men go. He'd worked at the local Ingle's for longer than most cared to remember, and had succeeded because he didn't have to think. "When Hap starts thinking, the world isn't safe," Cleo said.

"Hapless sounds more like it," Georgeann said, then apologized for poking fun in church, though it was the basement and not the sanctuary.

Hap, as Cleo had explained early on, wasn't his real name. He'd been christened "Harold James," but was nicknamed "Hap" as a life-long wink at his serious, nitpicky disposition. Even as a child he had earned a Boy Scout badge for a tidy room.

Sharing stories was the Busy Bees' forte. They seldom talked quilt patterns or about the work at hand because they'd been doing it so long. Why they could almost stitch with their eyes closed! Cleo, Bernice and Georgeann had once taken a course in quilt basics, then invited Marjorie, who liked to sew. Shortly after that, Georgeann invited her hairdresser, Shirleen, and Cleo asked her neighbor, Eva, to make an even half-dozen.

As a team, the women dusted off the old wooden quilt frame which had been in storage and began their sojourn of weekly quilting bees. The close-knit group had hung together for ten years and three months, a feat Cleo considered almost spiritual. "You're my sisters," she said, though her comment made some eyes roll, particularly Georgeann's, who stiffened whenever Cleo implied that they were social equals. Had it not been for quilting, they would have nothing in common—a banker's wife and a former checkout clerk—but she could no more resist Cleo's stories than the rest of the group.

Last month, Cleo topped her own storytelling when she related how their hot water heater had gone on the blink and Hap had decided to fix it.

"He's always doing that, a regular Mr. Fixit who doesn't know the first thing about mechanics."

The other women sighed and smiled to one another, secretly pleased they didn't have such a mate to contend with, though Shirleen, a widow, said a husband like Hap would be better than none at all. "You don't know what you've got until you've lost him," she said, which sent a sobering chill around the room. "Why else would I stand on my feet all day fixing women's hair?"

The others offered sympathetic nods.

"Why doesn't he get a hobby like my Woodrow?" Georgeann asked. "He collects old coins."

Cleo shrugged. "What does a grocer do, collect old food?"

"I've heard that vintage labels are valuable," Bernice offered.

Cleo clipped a thread close to the fabric. "There's no way Hap would collect anything."

"Are you kidding? He keeps you around," Eva said.

The group chuckled.

"No girls," Cleo said as she rethreaded her needle, "Hap says his hobby is keeping me straight." The white thread was waxed to glide through the layers of fabric, but its stiffness made it unruly to handle, even for experienced fingers.

Eva, a rounded figure with steel-wool hair, agreed. She was a retired schoolteacher whose husband, Dick, a former fireman, was the ultimate couch potato mainly because he seared his lungs years ago in a fire which left him disabled. "All he does is watch old movies and keep tabs on me. I have to lock the bathroom door to get any privacy."

"Be glad you have a man to keep you company," Shirleen said. Tall and spare with a jet-black hairdo wrapped into the shape of a hornets' nest, she sewed the tiniest stitches in the group. In her lonely existence, she'd had plenty of time to practice. "I can't wait to sit down in the evening and prop my feet up," she said, "and I can't stand not having something to do with my hands." She hadn't considered stitching for the community until Georgeann called her to join the Busy Bees.

"I'll second that one," Marjorie said. They all knew how her ex had left her for his secretary. It was an old story, a cliché, but one they bore with Marjorie as she sorted out her life, and with their listening ears, helped her get back on her feet. "Quilting is my salvation," she concluded. "You girls are like family."

When she said it, the women looked around the table and nodded to one another, fearful of walking in any of their shoes. Marjorie was usually the first to arrive and the last to leave, craving each moment, trying to find excuses to be in a crowd. She had joined three church committees at a time to fill up her calendar and attended most any receiving in the evening hours, whether she knew the deceased or not. The only quilting she did was during Guild meetings.

A hapless husband might seem endearing to the lonely, but Cleo didn't see it that way. She'd been charmed by her husband back when they were young. Hap was the handsome stock boy when she joined Ingle's to work checkout. A few years later, she quit work to stay home and start a family while Hap stayed on, eventually graduating to head stock man, then produce manager and finally, assistant manager. He had a friendly face, though none of the quilters would bother to ask him where to find ingredients for lemon meringue, tomato aspic or beef ragout. He wouldn't know any more about those things than how to piece a crazy quilt.

"He's still a stock boy at heart," Cleo said. "He can't stand anything out of order. He'll go through the linen closet and arrange towels and sheets by color and type."

"I could put him to work," Shirley said. The rest of the group agreed that having Hap around would be like a live-in butler. What woman wouldn't appreciate a fellow who picks up after himself?

"If he does windows, send him my way," Marjorie said. Everyone knew her place could use some sprucing up, but assumed her dim eyesight made her less conscious of the mess.

"Some days I'd be glad to oblige," Cleo said, then quickly added, "He could've gone into management with a chain store, but he said it would be too many nights and weekends. He'd rather have time to enjoy the family."

"Such a sweet man," Shirleen said.

For years, everyone wondered how Hap Hudson managed supporting himself, a wife and three daughters as grocery clerk. But anyone who knew Cleo realized that her thrift and efficiency were key.

"My girls are successful," Cleo said, "but they never got the hang of threading a needle."

"That's because you're so good at it," Bernice said, slipping her own needle into a patch of blue fabric.

"Girls these days don't sew anything," Georgeann added. "Who takes Home Ec anymore? It's a wonder that Tex Tiles is still in business."

Tex Tiles, a Carolinas legend, was a supermarket of fabrics, notions, trims, fluffy battings corralled in wire bins—everything one could possibly need for a sewing project. All of the Busy Bees were quilt purists, insisting that nothing but pure cotton comprise the pieced tops and backing, though they would occasionally cave in to using polyester batting—except Shirleen. She counted her pennies unless they involved quilt batting. "I'll pay the extra five dollars for solid cotton. That other stuff has too much loft," she said.

Cleo had told them how Hap, in a fit of creative energy, had once placed firecrackers around the perimeter of their attic as fire insurance.

"Fire insurance?" Marjorie said. She nearly fell onto the quilt frame where she was stitching the outline of a large diamond.

"He said if the firecrackers went off, we'd know the house was on fire," Cleo said.

Shirleen rolled her eyes. "Now I've heard it all."

"Now don't you girls mention this to anyone," Cleo said. "I don't want Hap to hear that I've told you. He already knows that I consider it a bone-headed idea."

"I don't know," Eva said. "If smoke alarms weren't available, it might make perfectly good sense." She was the left-handed quilter in the group, a spinster who reveled in being independent and creative. She once sewed a three-dimensional "art quilt" using ladies' undergarments—bra snaps, girdle fasteners, old hosiery, garter belts. It was the talk of the town when she displayed it at a local art show, though Georgeann and Bernice insisted she not credit the Busy Bees for such crassness.

"Better those old garter belts are on that quilt than cutting into my legs," Marjorie rubbed her own thick calf. She switched to slacks years ago and offered up her ditched dresses for quilt fabric, a possibility that floundered when the Bees sniffed polyester blend.

When it came to zany stories, Cleo took the prize. At their last meeting, she shared how Hap once hooked a drip hose up to the water heater, snaked it out to the patio and let it drain into her firethorn bushes. "They were beautiful in the spring with their white flowers and in the fall with red berries. Thanks to Hap, the hot water cooked the roots."

Marjorie shook her head as she measured a length of quilting thread. "That's the craziest one I've heard yet."

"I have a firethorn growing outside our front entryway," Bernice said. "Woodrow trained it to branch straight out on both sides like a Jerusalem cross."

"It sounds like he does more than count coins," Shirleen said.

Cleo, as always, steered the conversation back her way. "Can you imagine him throwing hot water on it?"

"If he were my husband, I'd scald him myself," Marjorie said in her bitter divorcee voice.

The rest of nodded like bobbing dog figures in a rear window.

"He thought it would be good to water them. I had might as well have set fire to them," Cleo said, "or used a blow torch."

And she was right. Those bushes have dropped so many leaves, it was doubtful that they would survive.

Hap's misadventures had cost him plenty. Several years earlier, he sideswiped a mailbox, which left an unsightly crease along the quarter panel and the passenger door of their Impala. The Busy Bees noticed it when Cleo drove to quilting circle one Tuesday. The car clunked around wounded for several weeks before Hap said he'd have it fixed. Instead of taking the car to a body shop, he drove it to the Main Street Exxon and had the attendants bang on it for a while; but after paying them a hundred dollars, the door still creaked and needed repainting.

"Whoever heard of a gas station doing body work?" Cleo asked. After paying Exxon, she eventually had to take the car to a body shop and pay two hundred dollars, thus adding insult to injury.

And then there was the time Home & Garden TV convinced Hap that their roof needed cleaning. What better way to use up the marked-down bleach he'd bought home from the store? "He'll keep something like that around only if *he* foresees a use for it," Cleo explained.

This was right after he used part of his savings to lay new carpet, she told the group that Hap filled a garden sprayer with bleach solution and carried the snake-nozzled contraption through the living room, up the stairs, into the hallway and their master bedroom. He was out on the upstairs deck over the porch before he realized what had happened: he'd drizzled bleach all over the carpet.

When I returned home, he was down on his hands and knees trying to fill the light spots with a felt-tip marker," Cleo said.

"That would be enough for me," Marjorie sputtered. "I'd call a divorce lawyer."

Six months later, the spots remained, reminding Cleo every time she vacuumed that she should've been home tending to housework instead of quilting. "To top it all off, the bleach shriveled all of my annuals I'd put out in their flower boxes and along the sidewalk, right under the drip line of the roof," she said.

The plants struggled to come back, but all they did was sputter and wilt. "It was a total waste of forty dollars and fifty cents because my knuckle-brained husband didn't warn me to cover them."

"Couldn't you replace them?" Georgeann suggested.

"I'd replace *him*," Marjorie insisted. "There's nothing more depressing than dead flowers."

Cleo sighed. "If I go back to the nursery to buy more, what are the chances they'll have any left to match?"

"About as much of a chance of finding fabric of the same dye lot once you've started a quilt," Bernice said, and they could all relate to that problem. More than once, Cleo had come to the rescue with her trove of old fabrics—a calico library big enough to blend with, if not match, any color imaginable.

For years, Cleo had made dresses for all of her girls; so she'd accumulated a lot of scraps and hid them in her laundry room cupboards, out of sight. Whenever the quilting guild began a new pattern, Cleo would check to see if she has enough of one color or another, and she usually did because she'd kept everything sorted by color in boxes in her laundry room. She was one of the fortunate women who had an actual room for her sewing and laundry, with a fold-out ironing board Hap installed during one of his Fix-It weekends, and a deep sink to soak lingerie and enough cabinets to store all of her detergents. Hap would bring dented boxes and shopworn bottles home; and Cleo had found a place to store them, and over time, supplied the Busy Bees with a few. In fact, Hap had saved up enough Soilax to wash their entire house—which he did, dressed up in a hat, goggles and long-sleeved shirt. Then he picked up a long-handled broom and cleaned every bit of dirt off the vinyl siding. The house looked like new construction.

"Whoever heard of washing the outside of your house?" Cleo asked.

The other women agreed that it was unusual.

She missed Quilter's Guild that week, saying she had to stay a step ahead of him with a tarp, covering her plants around the house so they wouldn't be damaged again.

"It was like keeping ahead of a bulldozer," she said later. "Hap wanted it to be a surprise, getting rid of those black streaks on the roof. Some surprise that was!"

Shortly afterwards, the group heard about the yellow jackets nested in a storm drain out at the end of the Hudsons' driveway. Hap had run into them mowing and was bound and determined to get rid of them for good.

"I told him, 'You need to spray them after the sun goes down,'" Cleo said, "and Hap said, 'How can you see what you're doing when it's dark?' so I suggested that he get some insecticide. Then Hap said, 'I never use fancy chemicals. Gasoline is the only thing that will eliminate ground bees.' I was sure he'd set fire to the yard."

She might as well have saved her breath. The next day, she heard him puttering around in the garage, then start up their patched-up Chevrolet and drive slowly out to the end of the driveway and aim a squirt gun out the window. "I asked him what he was trying to do and he said, 'Kill some bees.'"

"I knew right then and there I'd heard it all," she shook her head. "I could imagine gasoline dripping onto the seats and the car smelling like a filling station for weeks—which it did."

"There's no easy way to remove that odor," Georgeann said. "I hate when Woodrow isn't around to pump gas for me."

No one thought Cleo would ever divorce Hap; but last week, she came as close as she had come in her forty years of married wilderness.

The next meeting day, the quilting circle gathered as usual in the basement; and it wasn't long until she dragged herself through the door, her head hanging low, her shoulders slumped.

"I've reached the last straw," she said sadly. Hap had been on a cleaning binge to get ready for the Emmanuel fundraiser. "Last Tuesday while I was over here he poked through every closet, every drawer," she said, "and he had a bonfire doing out back all day, burning old boxes, newspapers and other trash. Then he came to the laundry room; he cleaned the place out, including all my fabrics."

"Kill him!" Marjorie said.

"Believe me, I thought about it," Cleo said. "He told me there was no use keeping these old rags. Rags! There he was,

147

with my calicos, florals, ticking stripes, solids, my whole Blue Willow collection."

A collective gasp swept around the quilt frame.

"That's horrible," Bernice said, a frown creasing her usual smile.

The women knew all of the fabrics from one time or another. It felt as if they had lost old friends.

"It was too late for Mama's flour sack towels," Cleo said, tears streaming down her cheeks. "Sixty-year-old material . . . destroyed."

"Why that's like throwing your Mama out!" Shirleen said, and others clucked their tongues. Loss of vintage cloth was too much to bear.

The Busy Bees gathered around Cleo, hugging her for her loss, and theirs too—to think that her entire stock of cotton had been roasted into nothingness. Losing that trove of pure cotton yard goods was a disaster. From now on, they would have to delve into their own meager supplies, maybe go out to Tex Tiles and buy the hard-to-find cottons they didn't have though they'd have to pay as much as seven dollars a yard. That would really hurt.

"I'm leaving," Cleo said.

"Leaving?" Eva said, rubbing the fingers of her left hand.

Georgeann's tweezed eyebrows rose to her hairline. "Not the Busy Bees."

"No, I'm leaving Hap." From her teary-eyed look, the women could tell that Cleo was upset. "He knew good and well that fabric wasn't rags. Who stores their rags in labeled boxes by color?"

The women all agreed that the notion was preposterous, but the thought of Cleo leaving her husband was a shock to them all. Hearing of his clownish misadventures over the years, they had come to think of him as light entertainment; but then none of the women had to experience them firsthand.

"He's so spiteful and mean," Cleo said.

No one could quibble with that statement; but this was hardly the time to totally agree, either.

"I don't blame your being upset," Georgeann said, "but you have to think this through. He's a good provider, a good father and husband."

"He stuck by you all these years," Bernice added.

"All these years," Cleo echoed. "You'd think he would at least respect my property. Ask before he tosses things away." She flung her arm over her shoulder.

The quilters gathered round like worker bees fanning their queen, watching Cleo, thin, helpless and vulnerable, melting in sobs in her mint-colored top with her "I'd Rather Be Quilting" pin on her left shoulder. They exchanged glances, wondering who would break the awkward silence.

"Pshaw," Shirleen broke the spell. "You don't want to leave your man and you sure as hell don't want to live alone."

Bernice and Eva gasped.

"Maybe Shirleen's right." Georgeann fondled her own wedding band. "You can always find more fabric, but God made only one Hap."

Marjorie nodded in agreement, though she didn't wear jewelry.

The Bees eyed one another in agreement. Of the six, only three had husbands, not that they wouldn't choose one—even a bonehead—if it were up to them.

"Hap's been such a good provider, and a good father," Georgeann said. "Think where you'd be without him."

"You never realize what you've got until it's gone," Shirleen said.

"You can say that again," Marjorie agreed.

Cleo looked at the kindly faces with their roadmap wrinkles from life's trials, joys and celebrations. They would stand behind her like batting stitched into her skin, friends who've helped plan and stitch masterpiece quilts, swapped ideas, shared stories, and, most importantly, laughed at her own frustrations. A look of peace washed over her face as Shirleen handed her a tissue. It was a kindness from one who'd known loss far more tragic than bundles of roasted fabric.

"We can always buy fabric, can't we, girls?" Bernice said.

They nodded.

"Things aren't so bad that they can't be worse," Bernice said as she hugged Cleo. "What's a few pieces of old cloth?"

"But this is my life. He's jealous of my Tuesday mornings with you girls. He did it deliberately." Cleo dabbed her eyes.

The group stood as silent witness to her pain: Georgeann and her faded debutante beauty, Bernice's well-earned wrinkles, Shirleen's aching calves, Eva's arthritic fingers and Marjorie's near-sighted eyes—a well-threaded sisterhood toughened by endurance. Somehow, Cleo would overcome this rough patch.

"If you ask me, Hap was only being himself," Bernice said, ushering Cleo to her usual place at the quilt frame.

She leaned toward Cleo and whispered something into her ear—something none of the rest of them could hear—and then with a faint smile, she said, "Let's get to work."

Rebecca Lee Williams

The True Beauty

It all started one afternoon when I went to pick up my granddaughter from her sitter. My daughter, Maggie, was working late again; and, as always, it was Mamoo to the rescue. I didn't mind. As a matter of fact, I loved spending time with little Ann Marie. It took my mind off my empty house and the loneliness I felt after the recent passing of my husband, Nelson. I may be sixty-four, but I am by no means a Granny. I told Maggie when Ann Marie was born, that I wanted her to call me Mamaw. But all she could manage to get out of that tiny mouth was Mamoo, and that's how I came to be—the one and only Mamoo Jean.

My car pulled into the driveway of Emma Landon's house, and out burst Ann Marie through their breeze-way. She was in tears as she came over to meet my car.

"What's wrong, sweetie?" I asked as she crawled into the backseat.

"Miss Emma said my momma was ugly," she sobbed.

"She said what!" I yelled.

I turned so sharply to comfort Ann Marie, that I darn near strangled myself on the seatbelt. I cannot tell you the amount of pain and anger I felt at that moment. Here was my precious and innocent grand-baby, dealing with something so hurtful, and down-right mean. That little girl worshiped her momma so much. Emma was a nimble-minded fool, to tell that child that her momma was ugly. Oh, it burned me to the core. To top it off,

151

this woman was talking about *my* baby. No one talks about any of my children that way. No, sir! I was fixing to unclip my seatbelt when Ann Marie sensed my extreme distress.

"Please don't say anything Mamoo. Momma likes Miss Emma and I like her too . . . most days."

How could this five year old be so forgiving? I know how. She gets it from her Christian, well-educated and sincere momma; that's how. I supposed my daughter had already had that conversation with Ann Marie about how you need to cope with mean people in this world, about how that shouldn't turn you into a mean person. That sounds like my daughter, the lawyer that she was.

Maggie is the oldest of my two beautiful children. Maggie is now 35; and my son, John, is 31. For the record, they are *truly* beautiful. John, had the kind of smile that made women melt. Except for me that is, I remember that little deviant smile whenever something around the house was missing or broken. He moved away to California last year for an honest-to-goodness modeling career. I wasn't happy at first; but after he showed me how much he earned in one weekend from posing in his Hanes, I couldn't argue anymore.

Both Maggie and John were blessed with their daddy's tall and toned physique. I passed down my good cheek bones and thick wavy hair. My momma was a tall, broad, and strong Appalachian woman. She had a grip of steel from all those years of doing laundry by hand and picking tobacco on her family's farm. It was a good firm hand that she didn't mind sharing with your backside if you dared to cross her. Momma ruled with an iron fist, but she had no choice. She was widowed with three young children by the time she was 28. My daddy had slipped off a footbridge and drowned in the Clinch River on his way home Christmas Eve. Momma never remarried. She did grow a wicked temper over the years. But through it all, she loved us deeply. She was stern because she cared. We were all she had left in this world. Through her love, we learned to steer clear of the bad, and embrace the good.

When Maggie was born, my momma was so proud. She stayed with Nelson and me for almost a month. Here I was a new mother, and Momma hardly gave me a moment to hold my own baby! She rocked Maggie, washed diapers, cooked meals and was the happiest I had seen her in twenty years.

"Good golly," Momma used to say, "look at that baby eat! You mark my words, she'll grow as big as an oak tree someday. Takes after her Granny, she does."

Momma was right. Maggie did grow big and strong. In her high school days, Maggie was the Anna Kournikova of her tennis team. Emma Landon was also on the tennis team. Emma's involvement included picking out the chic tennis skirts rather than breaking a sweat with a racquet. I always thought Emma envied Maggie. My daughter was the one bringing home the trophies while Emma was the one posing pretty for the local sports reporter.

How could Emma say such a horrible thing about my Maggie? Maggie trusted this woman to honestly care for her young daughter. I wanted to know so badly what had brought this on. Actually, what I really wanted to do was go inside that house and give that woman "what for" with both fists. Instead, I composed myself, but not before sending a burning glare into Emma's living room window from my driver's seat. I handed Ann Marie a tissue, then drove us down to the Frosty Cone, where we both sat in silence sipping strawberry shakes.

My mind tells me we were both trying to figure out the same thing. Should we tell Maggie what happened? As we slurped up the last little bit of shake, I think we both came to same conclusion, which was no. I did tell Ann Marie that if Miss Emma said one more hateful thing about her, her family, or anyone she knew, I was to know about it. It would be our little secret . . . that is, until the sheriff found Miss Emma lying in the ditch outside her house.

We arrived back at my home. Aside from the after-school incident at Miss Emma's, Ann Marie proceeded to tell me about her joyful day in Kindergarten. If Nelson was here, he would prop Ann Marie up in his lap; then they'd both munch on peanuts. He kept that can of planters on the side table by his big recliner. Nelson would smile while Ann Marie chattered on and on. He loved to hear her little stories. Nelson would have driven his truck clear into Miss Emma's living room had he known what she said about his Maggie.

"Mamoo, what's for dinner?" Ann Marie asked, as she dragged a kitchen chair over to my counter to get a better look.

"Oh, I don't know, dumplin'. Mamoo was thinking maybe barbeque and beans."

"I don't like that sticky ol'barbeque. Can I have a hot dog instead?"

Oh, to have that youthful metabolism. Ann Marie was a walking string bean. She could stand to gain a few pounds, in my opinion. I, too, have my days when I crave a good hot dog, and it looks like today was the day.

"Hotdogs it is," I agreed.

Ann Marie gleefully hopped down from the chair and went over to the fridge to pull out the hot dogs. I opened up a can of pork-n-beans, and then started to mince up some onions. Ann Marie enjoyed plopping the hot dogs down into the pot of water. The splashes covered my stove top but I didn't care. It's funny how grandparenthood changes your philosophy on parenting. Now if that was my son, John, making a mess on my stove, I would have hollered. But this time around it's my granddaughter; she's having fun; and my life is much more at ease than when I was trying to raise my own children. We were too busy cooking and giggling in the kitchen to notice that Maggie had come in.

"Hey! What's going on in here?" Maggie smiled.

She took off her overcoat and put her briefcase down on the table. Maggie rolled up her sleeves and joined us at the counter.

Then Maggie's cell phone rang. I could tell by the sweetness in her voice, she was talking to her husband, Donnie. Maggie's husband, Donnie, was a civil engineer for the highway department. He had spent this week away working on the interstate expansion up north. He was a good daddy, and I was pleased to know Maggie had a good man in her life.

" . . . she's helping Momma make supper. I don't know. Looks like hot dogs. Okay. Call you back after bath-time. We love you too." Maggie clapped her phone shut.

"Listen, Momma." Ann Marie whispered. "When you squeeze the ketchup bottle just like this, it makes a poot sound." Ann Marie used all her might to squeeze out the remaining dab of ketchup from the bottom of the bottle. It did make a loud "poot" sound crazy enough to be a whoopy-cushion and we all stood there laughing and leaning on each other. After a little while, we put the dogs in their buns, and sat down to eat.

"Oh, gosh, Mom! I almost forgot to show you something."

Maggie opened her briefcase and fished around inside for something. She beamed as she pulled out the latest edition of *Oprah* magazine. She handed it to me.

"Turn to page 214," Maggie said.

I squinted to find the page numbers and clumsily thumbed my way to page 214. Then I sat up straight in my chair, astonished.

"My Lord, Maggie! Is that you?"

"Yes, Momma, it is me."

I couldn't believe my eyes. There was a photograph of my daughter's gorgeous face, big as life. She looked incredible. I could feel tears welling up in my eyes. I was so proud.

"How did this happen?" I asked.

"Remember when I asked you to watch Ann Marie for that long weekend? I told you that Donnie and I needed a little time away?"

"Uh huh," I gulped.

"Well, what happened was this. The cosmetic company that I've been using for years put out an ad one day looking for customer contestants to enter their beauty contest. Well, I called John and when I told John about it, he said 'go for it'. So I did. Then weeks went by and I thought there's *noooo* way I'd ever have a chance of winning. I didn't even tell Donnie what I'd done. Then one day, I got a letter saying they wanted me to come to Memphis for a photo shoot. So we went down there . . . and there you have it. They picked me. Can you believe it? They picked *me!*"

"Waaahhooow," Ann Marie groaned, her mouth filled with bun.

The cosmetic company's full page ad in the magazine said it all. There was a quote beside Maggie's face that read, "I've been a customer for years. The products make you feel good about yourself. And when you feel good about yourself, you can face anything that comes your way."

"Honey, do you mind if I show this to Miss Emma, the next time I see her?" I asked as Ann Marie and I exchanged winks.

"Sure, Momma," Maggie said between bites, "be my guest."

I sighed a tremendous sigh and clutched that magazine to my chest. I looked up at the ceiling and silently thanked the Good Lord and Nelson. I knew he must have had a hand in this. I now had all the ammunition I needed to get back at that cold-hearted Emma Landon. After supper, I was going to tuck away my ammo, that Oprah magazine, in the glove compartment of my car, for safe keeping. Knowing that one day, I would pull it out and parade it in front of her face. Shoot, if I had my way, I'd wallpaper Emma's front door with my baby's gorgeous photograph. But right now, I'll just enjoy my hot dog and be proud of the blessings seated at my table.

Susanna Holstein

Burning the Trash

"Who will get this place when I'm gone?" Emma thought to herself. "I'm eighty-two, and my old bones are wearing out."

She looked out the window at the dawning April day. This was always her favorite time of year, and she looked forward to the new green of grass and trees, and the brightness of daffodils and forsythia against the backdrop of the softening outline of the mountains. Folks told her she needed to move to town, but she intended for her last breath to be the air from this West Virginia hill farm.

Now she faced the reality of having to write her will. It seemed like something that could wait, until on this morning of her birthday. How had she gotten so old? Time had passed so quickly; each day there was the familiar rhythm of milking, caring for the cows and chickens, getting in wood for the stove. And suddenly she was an old woman, and it was past time to be deciding what to do with the farm.

Death didn't frighten her. She believed firmly in Heaven and lived her life accordingly. The warmth of hellfire sometimes seemed appealing when her joints ached in the mornings; though, she thought with a smile, "Sorry Lord, I'm just kidding. I'm staying on the straight and narrow."

She poured her coffee and looked at the budding lilac bush outside the window. She had a lot of nieces and nephews, and there was one who she thought would appreciate the old place and give it the care it deserved. She had always been fond of Caroline, her youngest niece. She nodded, picked up pen and paper, and began to write.

I, Emma Parsons, being of sound mind and body . . .

Later that day, Caroline and her husband Edrow came to visit, carrying a big chocolate cake and birthday card. Emma was delighted to see them. "Caroline never forgets my birthday," she thought. "I've made the right choice. I don't know Edrow that well, but he seems like a nice enough boy. They've been married now for a couple of years and I haven't seen anything out of the way about him. I think they'll like this place."

Later that evening she showed Caroline her will. The girl hugged Emma, laughing.

"Oh, Aunt Emma, you are a real sweetie. You know I love this place."

Caroline and her husband visited more regularly after that, and Edrow began to look at the place with a proprietary air. During their visits to Emma he discussed his plans for the house and property once Emma was gone.

"We might just bulldoze down this old place," he said one evening. "It's got no insulation or foundation. No one would buy it. I sure wouldn't want to live in it. This land is valuable, too. We could divide it into lots and make a killing." Caroline looked down at the oilcloth table cover and said nothing.

Emma listened and watched them both, her lips set in a hard line. This place, this farm, had been her life's work. She knew each and every plant in her flower garden, had planted them all from starts given to her by friends. She'd strung every inch of fence, built the barn, and filled the cellar house every year with the produce of the garden. It was home, a cherished place that needed to be nurtured. It was not an investment opportunity.

The next evening the young couple visited again. Emma greeted them on the porch and invited them to the kitchen for coffee. She slowly filled the pot, emptying the old grounds into the overflowing trash can. Caroline sat at the table and talked about local news, but Ed's eyes were moving speculatively around the room, taking in the cast iron wood cook stove, high-back enameled sink and jelly cupboards. His eyes did not register approval of what he saw.

"Ed, dear, would you take this trash to the old barrel out back and burn it? I missed the trash man this morning, and it will smell bad by next week." Emma smiled at the young man, and he looked startled at the interruption of his thoughts.

Edrow sighed, put down his coffee cup and got to his feet. "Sure, Emma. Got any matches?"

She searched on top of the refrigerator, found a box and handed it to him, smiling. "You're a dear. Thank you!"

Edrow grabbed the bag and pushed open the screen door out to the porch. Emma watched him walking across the yard to the barrel. A match flared in the half-dark, silhouetting Edrow as his stood with folded arms in front of the flames. Emma turned back to Caroline.

"Let me fix you something to eat, dear." Emma opened the refrigerator and reached in to take out leftover barbecue as Edrow stomped back into the kitchen.

"That porch is an accident waiting to happen," Edrow complained. "My foot darn near went through it there in the center. I can't wait to get this firetrap torn down and the land graded out so we can get it subdivided."

"What makes you think you're going to be able to do that, Ed? I'm still kicking, last time I checked."

"You know what I mean, Aunt Emma. This place is going to be ours . . ."

"Why are you so sure of that?"

"It's in your will, that's why. You said it would be ours . . ." He stopped, staring at Emma.

Emma laughed. "My will? I don't have a will anymore. You just burned it with that trash. Now this place will go into heirship.

159

You know I have a lot of other nieces and some nephews too. It will probably take years to get it all sorted out."

She sat back gently in her rocking chair. "More coffee, Edrow dear?"

Donna Akers Warmuth

Fine Ways

On the day their car had been hit by the Norfolk and West-ern train, Jimmie Lou and Muriel Atkins were driving home from their weekly hair appointment at Tangles and Java. Even though it was a tragic accident, Laura McCall found herself praying for patience as "Bringing in the Sheaves" pushed up to the rafters of Lawson's Funeral Home chapel where mourners wished farewell to the two Atkins sisters.

Laura muttered to her sister, Rachel Snead, "I'm not sure it's appropriate to play a recording of them singing their own gospel songs at their funeral." The spinster sisters, Jimmie Lou and Muriel Atkins, were locally prominent gospel singers in the region. Their best selling recording, "Stalked by the Holy Ghost," had actually ranked number 157 on the Holy Hit List.

"Each had asked that the other sister sing at her funeral. Since both died at the same time, I reckon it seemed the right thing to do," Rachel whispered back to Laura.

Taking their place in the line to pay respects at the two identical pink caskets, Laura again nudged Rachel, "I don't understand why those two tried to race the train at the crossing in that ancient Cadillac. Maybe they had too much coffee at that Curls and Café hair salon, or whatever it's called."

The singing continued, the nasal voices sailing from the speakers, like a siren song summoning their owners to awaken. Family, friends, and stragglers with nothing better to do on

161

Saturday afternoon, dabbed at teary, blurry, or allergy-irritated eyes. Everyone marveled at the demure smiles never seen on Emily and Muriel in life, now perpetually frozen like cake icing on their still faces. Laura maintained that as you grow older, attending funerals becomes dangerous to your health, and she attended enough already in her 74 years. Like meeting a third cousin on Main Street whom you haven't seen in years—you always bump into your own mortality at wakes and funerals. One of the few benefits to attending funerals were the free plastic hair bonnets, so handy in a sudden downpour to protect your hair-do.

The heady aroma of funeral flowers clinging to their clothes made Laura feel nauseated as they left the chapel. Rachel and Laura then eased their elderly frames into Laura's Ford LTD.

"We had better shake a leg to make it to Eliza's house on time."

Rachel turned beseeching blue eyes to Laura. "I don't guess we have time to run through Tastee-Freeze for a fish sandwich?"

"If there isn't a long line at the drive-through."

Laura smiled and mused to herself it would take a large amount of food to satisfy her sister. Rachel resembled a plump hen sitting on a nest, with her ample stomach forming a pillow over her legs.

As the line at Tastee-Freeze drive-through inched along, Laura thought about all three of their lives as widows. Forging a new tradition since Rachel's husband died, the three sisters met for tea, hot in the winter and iced in the summer, on the fourth Saturday of each month. The meeting had settled at Eliza's house, because she had more room. Truthfully, she enjoyed going to Eliza's house, a white Georgian with noble columns, because she liked to pretend that it was her house for just an afternoon.

"Those new heart pills I'm taking make me hungry all the time. This is just what I needed to tide me over at Eliza's house."

Rachel bit into her sandwich and scattered crumbs over her purple polyester skirt.

"I prefer to save some room for those mini-quiches she serves," Laura sniffed with a hint of disdain for fish sandwiches.

On the drive back to "Snob Knob," Eliza's neighborhood, Laura considered Eliza's perfect life. The youngest of the three girls, Eliza always tried to do everything better than her sisters. To everyone, it seemed that Eliza's marriage to Charles Jameson was her greatest triumph.

"Do you remember that Momma always told Eliza her good looks would bring her luck in life? And Eliza bartered her looks for a life full of ease with Charles Jameson. Who would have thought her life with him would have turned into such a lie?" Laura spoke her thoughts out loud to Rachel without realizing it.

In her youth, a girl's beauty could rescue her from a life of poverty; and their family had been dirt poor. It was only after Charles's death last year that the mirage of Eliza's contentment and happiness had ended, at least to others.

"You always think Eliza's life was easy, but she had her share of troubles, too, just different that the kind we had. They did raise three wonderful children, who all went to college," Rachel said.

Driving her aged LTD into Eliza's fancy neighborhood, filled with Cadillacs and Mercedes, always made Laura feel as if she were trespassing. As she swung the car carefully into Eliza's driveway, Laura recalled the shock for Eliza at Charles's estate settlement.

"He sure had a lot of nerve by naming and giving money to his illegitimate children by Miranda Clark in his will, along with his three children by Eliza," mused Laura. It turned out that Charles Jameson, Esq. had kept plain Miranda Clark as a mistress for over 30 years.

"I think the worst of it was that since the will was recorded at the courthouse, everyone in town knows of Charles's other children," Rachel shook her head sadly.

"After all that, I don't know how Eliza held her head up in the aisles of the Piggly Wiggly," Laura sighed dramatically, but secretly didn't feel much pity for Eliza.

Eliza had known that Charles was up to something, but with her Pollyanna attitude, she had ignored the signs. "Here, have a piece of teaberry gum to cover up the fish sandwich on your breath. We don't want Eliza to know we stopped for lunch."

Laura parked near the fragrant rose bushes marching up Eliza's driveway like Her Majesty's guard. Without any regrets, she clipped a few bushes with her car's fender.

Rachel patted her stomach. "That was only an appetizer for me. I still have plenty of room for the morsels she serves."

Eliza opened the front door, and they briefly saw her blank face, like an empty hand puppet, before she tacked on a token smile. A tempting aroma of peanut butter cookies baking reached out the door and tickled their noses. The maid must have put cookies in the oven before she left for the afternoon.

"Why, Eliza, your hairdo is beautiful, honey! Now, are you still going to The Mane Event for your weekly rinse and set? I've heard their business has fallen off, since Todd, that sissy guy started fixing hair there. I still go there; but, of course, I see Denise. I always make sure to talk to him though; it keeps my mind open." Laura touched Eliza's silken curls.

Laura and Rachel tucked their arms in each of Eliza's limp arms. "Oh, how I wish you could have been at the Atkins sisters' funeral, it was just majestic," Laura continued. "When 'Stalked by the Holy Ghost' was played, I felt the funeral parlor shake; everybody was crying so hard."

Eliza looked away absently, "Well, I don't feel like being in large crowds, with my claustrophobia." She had developed a number of strange disorders after Charles's death, preventing her from leaving the house for days at a time.

"Honey, you wouldn't have enjoyed it. The loud music would have given you a headache," Rachel soothed.

Cutting her eyes left and right as they walked through the house, Laura marveled again at the grace and downright class, the almost Chanel No. 5 this house gave off. Sometimes she wished she and William could have lived in a house like this, instead of their tiny yellow bungalow, which probably smelled more like Jean Nate.

"Is this vase new? I saw one like it at Wal-Mart yesterday," Laura said, trying to get a rise from Eliza.

"Gracious no. I had to special-order the vase through my decorator." Eliza trailed her fingers lovingly over the vase and straightened the doily.

They settled aching joints into patient, cushioned rocking chairs in the sun porch, sipped the iced tea, and nibbled on quiches and cookies. Classical music, maybe by Bach or that man who went deaf, added to the relaxing atmosphere in Eliza's house. Small talk came easily among them, their high voices floating up in the humid air currents.

"Our garden did so well this year. I am overrun with green beans to can," Rachel complained. "Why don't I bring some tomatoes over for you, Eliza."

Eliza smiled on cue, not meeting their eyes.

"I put up 10 quarts of blackberry jam last week and brought you one. Let me get it out of the car before it gets too hot." Laura peered at Eliza's pale face with concern. Rachel tried to entertain Eliza with stories of her grandchildren. Sighing, Laura limped back through the house to get the jam from her car. That hip replacement surgery still had not restored her movement.

Always emotionally fragile, Eliza had a bout with nerves after Charles died. She also developed a hand-washing compulsion, I think her doctors called it, cleansing her hands up to 20 times a day. Both she and Rachel had visited Eliza every day to carry her through the first few weeks after Charles's death. Eliza's children even talked about committing her to the hospital in Roanoke again, where she went thirty years ago to get electric shocks for nerves, or depression as it's called now. But she and Rachel convinced Eliza's children to allow her more time to recover from her grief. Why, after the treatment thirty years ago, Eliza had forgotten her sisters' names and drooled for weeks.

Passing the entrance table, Laura fingered a silver box, monogrammed with Eliza's initials. In the early hours of the morning, when her sleep had edged surreptitiously away on leathery wings, Laura often thought about her sisters, their childhood, their late husbands and the way each of their lives had turned out. Both she and Rachel had married kind, loving men, although not as rich or as handsome as Eliza's Charles. Her William was a fast talker and a showman, but couldn't keep a penny in his pocket. But lord, how he had worshipped her — she reminisced to her sisters about how often he had often bought her flowers and massaged her feet each night. It is so humble and touching to see a powerful man bent over your feet, his head bowed as if in prayer.

Although she didn't tell them about the bad times with William, her sisters probably knew. Like the time the sheriff came in the middle of the night to arrest William, scaring the children with the flashing lights on his car. This town is so small that even if you hold your secrets close like a veil, they eventually slip out around the edges. As she returned from the car and stepped inside the grand doorway, Laura determinedly pushed those unpleasant memories aside and thought about Rachel's life.

Rachel had married Floyd Campbell, a poor dirt farmer, and worked her fingers to the bone, although their hilltop farm never did amount to much. Not counting the one time Floyd ran off to Kingsport and was picked up drunk and locked in the calaboose overnight, it seemed that Rachel and Floyd got along tolerably well. She drove Rachel all the way to Kingsport to bail out poor Floyd that time, and Eliza put up the bail money. If she had to choose the best husband from among her sisters, Laura believed Rachel had made the wisest choice, for Floyd would have done anything to make her happy. Early in their marriage, they established the ease of a well-worn house shoe, not worn enough to replace, but comfortable enough on your bunions.

As Laura sank back in her chair next to her sisters, she absently scratched under her Eva Gabor wig. Although wigs were handy to cover up limp hair the last few days before her next hair appointment, they could be mighty itchy in the summer.

"The tricks we used to play on each other! Remember when I hid a boiled egg in your Easter bonnet and you didn't find it until the next spring?" Rachel was trying to ease a smile from Eliza.

"That smell was awful—why didn't I find it before the next spring? The mothballs in the closet must have covered the rotting egg smell up," Eliza said, drinking her tea deeply and granting a chuckle.

"Well, we did have fun, but some of us worked hard too, helping with the cooking and farm work." Laura wanted to set things straight. "Sometimes I wish our grandchildren could have half the chores we had; it would build their characters better than Pokeman and Nintendo. Y'all know I had to help Mama with the cooking and biscuit making, so I didn't have time for playing like you two. I never saw two girls who resembled wild Indians so much in my life, always barefoot and scratched by brambles."

"Now Laura Anne, you know we did just as much work as you. And, for that matter, the reason you were inside so much is because you were always primping in the mirror above Papa's shaving bowl," admonished Rachel with a smile.

"That's right, Laura. You were Mama's favorite, and she let you get away with anything." Eliza slipped off her spectator pumps, and joined in the teasing. "Just because you made better biscuits than us, you thought you were the queen of the roost."

Laura could feel her blood pressure start to climb. Why did the two of them gang up and pick at her? Why couldn't they grow out of it by now?

"And, here we are, seventy-odd years later, fighting as usual. Now don't mind me, but I need to visit the powder room." Laura gingerly pulled herself up from her chair, adjusting her slip under her skirt. Incontinence was one of the more aggravating signs of aging, and hers was caused by having too many large babies. She heard Eliza's grandfather clock chime solemnly, almost agreeing with her about the passing minutes and years.

Seashells that looked as real as life graced the hand towels in the coral and gold decorated guest bathroom. She sniffed the scent from the plug-in air freshener, the ocean breeze fragrance to match the bathroom's motif. Laura preferred Country Garden scent air freshener in her bathroom.

Shaking her head, Laura considered her life. It had been a good one, these 74 years. Blessed by three good children and then doubly blessed with seven grandchildren, all in one life-time! And it didn't matter to her one bit that her eldest son had married an Eskimo woman—their children were the cutest, with those slanted eyes and pug noses. Certainly, she realized that her family might not have been able to stay together without her sisters' help. Rachel had provided Laura with a few cured hams each year, and Eliza sometimes had helped pay the light bill. After her marriage, she quickly learned that life is not a "bed of roses," as the old song goes. The one constant in her life had not been William, it had been her sisters.

Rejoining her sisters in the sunroom, Laura plucked a lemon bar from the plate and savored its delicate taste, sweet and sour. "I really do enjoy these Saturday teas—here we are together again, just like when we were growing up. It seems that the years in between childhood and now (filled with diaper changing, needy husbands, Girl Scout meetings, Tupperware parties) have faded away like an old black and white picture, as if that part of our lives never happened at all."

Rachel dropped a broccoli quiche into her mouth. "Why, raising our families took so much out of us. I dearly love my children, but they sucked the marrow right out of my bones."

"I feel like these old shells that we call bodies have served their purpose, bearing and raising children, and I am plumb give out," Eliza added. "Sometimes, in the breath of the wind, I seem to hear the Lord calling me home."

Laura exchanged a worried look with Rachel, and deftly switched the subject to the new Methodist minister's stuck-up wife.

Conversation rose and fell in placid rhythms between them, like ocean swells. Laura thought the most precious thing about talking with family, is that you don't have to think about what you say before you say it. You can talk raw right from the gut.

"Eliza, you need to be feeding this African violet, or it will up and die. And be careful about watering the leaves." Laura picked dead blooms off a plant near the window.

"Yes, I know I should pay more attention to my plants, I will mention it to the maid. I just don't feel like doing a thing anymore." Eliza mumbled, rocking slowly. "These peanut butter cookies were Charles's favorite. I made them every Saturday for him and his golfing buddies to carry on the course." Eliza nibbled a cookie, still warm from the oven.

Rachel and Laura caught each other's eyes and thought, "here we go again."

"Y'all know that I made sure he had one of the finest funerals this town has ever seen. The bagpipes playing "Amazing Grace" at the graveyard tore everybody up."

"Now Eliza, you just relax and remember the good times y'all had—all the traveling and your wonderful children," admonished Laura. It wasn't good to dwell on memories of

Charles with Eliza. She and Rachel didn't talk too much about their deceased husbands anymore.

"After the memorial service, they let me close his casket before loading it on the hearse. His face was arranged so differently, it was like saying goodbye to a stranger. So final, yet the heavy lid closed with hardly a sound at all," Eliza said dreamily.

The clock gonged again, carrying time along like a runaway horse.

Eliza rocked faster, and her eyes closed. A sigh sang through her thin shoulders. "I need to tell y'all something because I need somebody else to know. It has eaten away at me these past months, and I can't get any rest for the burden of it."

"Now Eliza, you just calm down—should I get one of your nerve pills for you?" Rachel shushed.

"No, I don't need a pill. Just listen to me. That day I came home from shopping, Charles was in his study, working as he usually did on Sundays. As I closed the front door, I heard a strange sound, a choking noise. I walked down the hall to his study and pushed open the door asking Charles if everything was all right. There he sat at his mahogany desk, his face beet red and pulling at his collar, gasping for air." Eliza smoothed her hair back into its bun and continued.

"He choked, 'Why are you just standing there like a knot on a log? Run and get me a heart pill from the bathroom.' And, I just stood, shocked, and watched him. I remembered the nights he didn't come home until late, the money he handed out to me and our children instead of love and attention, and the constant put-downs to me that I was just "white trash" and should feel lucky he married me. And, most of all, I thought about the gossip about Miranda Clark and her two children that I had endured so quietly and never let on like I knew. Watching him, clutching his heart, I just decided that it was between him and God this time and I wasn't going to interfere."

"Like it was a dream I had been anticipating my entire life, I just looked him right in the eyes, calmly shut his study door, and walked right back out of the house. I drove back to the mall, bought a black dress at Anne Taylor, and didn't return home for three hours. When I returned, he was dead, clutching his golf ball paperweight to his chest. You see, I shut the door on him and left him to die. Is that murder? And I still believe that I would do it again the same way. Then, I shut his casket door and sent him off to God for judgment." Eliza's head rested back on the rocker, but her hands still rubbed together restlessly.

Ticks from the clock and barks from the neighbor's dog formed a syncopation in the quiet. Laura and Rachel had stopped their rocking as they listened. When Eliza finished, they both started rocking again, as if on cue. Silence stretched between them as wide as a river.

Laura worried at her dentures with her tongue and thought about rights and wrongs, and just rewards. "Well, honey, Charles never did right by you, treated you like a rag door mat. I only found out about Miranda Clark a few years back, but didn't want to tell you for fear of hurting you. Bygones and all that. I don't hold your action against you at all; it wasn't murder. He turned his back on you and the children long ago, and he deserves the judgment that he will get from God."

"Eliza, he was dying, there was probably nothing you could have done anyway. I say let it go. Any woman who had to go through what you did would have done the same thing." Rachel caressed Eliza's delicate veined hand with her callused palm.

Eliza sighed, "You think? Y'all don't think I killed him? Will God hold that up to me at Judgment Day? I just needed to tell someone else, to share it with you, my sisters. Only you would understand why I closed the door."

Laura's mind vibrated in shock at her calm sister, and the secret she had nursed. She hadn't known things were so bad

171

between Eliza and Charles. In so many ways, Eliza's life had seemed perfect to everyone on the outside. Eliza always acted happy and cheerful. But, sometimes the brightest smiles hold the greatest pain. Well, now she wasn't alone with her secret and maybe she can make peace with it.

"Just let us help you shoulder this one, Eliza. That's what sisters are for." Laura nodded emphatically. There would be no more talk of that day. The sisters sipped their tea and chatted about the latest town gossip for the next half-hour, then quieted down like nesting doves.

Rachel heaved herself up from the chair, straightening her snug skirt. "Well, better get home, I got beans to shell for supper."

"Law, I need to clean up the house before my grandchildren come over and tear it right back up again." Laura pulled herself up by holding Rachel's hand.

Eliza graciously replied, "Don't y'all be rushing off—stay awhile. Stay and have some supper with me, there's plenty." In this town, you always offered visitors to stay for a meal, to be polite.

Murmuring their pressing excuses, Laura and Rachel gathered their white summer handbags, adjusting girdles and dentures. Hugs were exchanged as they stood in the honest July sun, exposing the wrinkles and worries that time had scratched on their faces. At the imposing front door, the three elderly widows held hands tightly, and Rachel's salt and pepper, Laura's blue, and Eliza's silver curls glowed like halos in the light.

Tammy Robinson Smith

Jewel Holler

Ruby's called us all here to Mommy's today. She must have some big news. Ruby's that way. Sometimes, I think she just likes the attention; but that's okay. It's not like she ever gits any attention from Big Jim; that's her husband. The only attention Big Jim ever gives is to hisself. Lord, that man does like to go on. If you don't know how much money he has, just ask him, he'll tell ya. And if you want to know how important he is in this county; just ask him, he'll tell ya; but that's just the way he is. Don't reckon he'll change at sixty-two years old, if he hasn't so far.

Ruby called me early this morning. Seems she'd already talked to Pearl and Garnet. Mommy sure did like them jewel names. She thought it was fitting since we lived at the end of Jewel Holler. Anyways, Ruby was right breathless and rushed when she was talking to me. She just told me to meet her and the sisters over here at Mommy's at lunchtime. She said she'd drive over to Abingdon and bring back a bucket of Kentucky Fried Chicken and all the fixin's. I said all right. I'm never one to turn down free food, and the Good Lord knows Ruby is generous— I'll give her that. She don't have one bit of trouble spending any of the money Big Jim's all the time bragging about.

That Big Jim, none of us never did see what Ruby saw in him. She dropped out of school when she was just fifteen years old to marry him. Lord, she should have known she'd spend the rest of her life listening to him talk. His people's all like that. Why, his daddy, Old Jim, the local jack-leg preacher, can drone on and on for days on end. Even though Mommy and Daddy went to church every Sunday, and Sunday evening, and back to Wednesday Prayer Meeting, they never went to Old Jim's tent revivals. Mommy always said it was nothin' more than a scam to separate God fearin' Christians from their offering to the Lord; which just went into Old Jim's back pocket more often than not.

Now, my husband, he's just the opposite. Don't speak if he ain't spoke to, and sometimes not even then. But he's a good man, my Johnny Jenkins is. We've been married thirty five years this coming May. Married him right out of high school, I did. I was the first in the family to graduate, since Ruby dropped out. Sure did make Mommy and Daddy proud. Of course, fat lotta good it did me. All's I've done since then is drop babies and raise them. Now, I'm babysitting grandyounguns while their mommies work at the sewing factory and their daddies in the mines; if at all. People complain about that sewing factory takin' all the women away from their children, but I'm telling ya', my youngest, Eileen, is making three dollars and seventy-five cents an hour as a supervisor on the day shift. Complain all you want, but that's good money in this county; better than most.

Lord, I swear, I wish Ruby would git here. My stomach's done eat through to my backbone. A chicken leg sure would hit the spot right about now. I know there ain't nothing in Mommy's refrigerator. We cleaned it out after the funeral last year, and split the leftovers between us all.

It's hard to believe Mommy is gone. We've not done anything to the house, other than give it a good cleaning the week after she died. Daddy died in '69. Mommy just carried on after he was gone, like the trooper she was. She was a good ole' girl; that's what she always called herself. Lord, I do miss her.

"Opal, Opal. Where are ya', honey? Come on out here to my car and help me git this chicken unloaded and into the house."

Lord, there's Ruby. Maybe now we'll git to the bottom of this big mystery; or at least git something to eat. I'm a' starving to death.

Walking through the living room, heading out to the front porch, it's hard to keep my eyes from tearing up as I'm hit with the familiar sights and smells of Mommy's living room. She always called it the parlor. She was so proud of the new furniture she got after Daddy died. It didn't take quite all of his miner's death benefit to bury him, what with our cousin Vernie working at the funeral home and all, and giving us a discount. So Mommy said that since it was the filth from the coal mine that had dirtied up her living room suite, she figured the least they owed her was some new furniture. We didn't argue with her, and secretly I agreed. Daddy could've at least sit on a towel or an old blanket when he got home of the evening, until he had time to git cleaned up; but he never did. Daddy wasn't a mean man by anyone's standards; just an inconsiderate one. I reckon he coulda' been worse. Lordy, lordy, lordy—how the time has passed. I can still see 'em both sittin' there in their chairs.

"Opal, just grab that bag with the soda pop in it, and git that bag of ice. I knew we'd need something to cool these drinks. Lord, it's a scorcher out here today. I bet it's eighty five degrees. Here, honey, let me git that car door."

Ruby bumps her generous behind against the car door of her shiny new Buick. Big Jim says nothing's too good for his wife. I've always thought he buys her a new car every year so everyone will know he can afford to. I swear, I know I should try harder to like him, considering how many years he's been married to my sister; but I just can't. Lord forgive, I just can't!

"Ruby, what in the world has you so all fired worked up this morning? I was planning on canning tomatoes today, but after

I got your call I just quit. I don't know why I fool with them anyway. Johnny won't eat them, and the younguns' would rather have a hamburger as any home cookin' anyway. I guess it's just borned in us to put up for the winter."

"Now, Opal, I'm not gonna say anything 'til Pearl and Garnet gits here. I'm just gonna tell y'all once, then, we ain't gonna talk about it anymore."

"Well, all right."

Ruby and me head into the house and back through the parlor to the kitchen. I don't know why she's being so ornery, but as long as I git to eat, I'm not gonna fuss with her over it. Besides, she did drive all the way over to Abingdon to the Kentucky Fried Chicken to git us this meal.

"Opal, it still hurts so bad when I look around this kitchen and think of all the meals Mommy prepared here for us and Daddy. It just all went by so fast. I never did think things would change, but they did. It was all over in the blink of an eye. The four of us as young girls, then marryin' and bringin' our babies home—then those babies growing up and marryin'. Lord, I've got great-grandchildren. How did that happen? It was all just in the blink of an eye. Now, I'm almost sixty years old. I've been married nearly forty-five years. Lord have mercy!"

"Ruby, you're not having one of them midlife crisis like the movie stars is always talkin' about are ya'? I declare, you've not gone Hollywood on me, have ya'?"

"Opal," Ruby laughs, "I'm just a' thinkin' out loud. Don't you ever just think out loud?"

"Not really."

Ruby keeps chuckling to herself as she turns around to open the cabinet above the kitchen sink.

"Do you mind if we use Mommy's plates to eat on, instead of the paper ones? I'll wash them up afterwards, if y'all don't want to."

"Why, sure, Ruby; that sounds like a fine idea. I'd like to eat off of Mommy's plates one more time."

Ruby turns to git the plates just as we hear an awful commotion outside.

"What in the world?" I exclaim as me and Ruby hustle back through the parlor to see what's going on.

Clank. Wheeze. Chortle. Cough.

"Aw, it's the very old devil!" We hear a familiar voice holler out through the open truck window.

It's Garnet and Pearl. We should have known.

"Garnet," Ruby hollers, "What in the name of common sense is going on?"

"Well, hello Pete! I can't help it if my car wouldn't start this mornin', and all I had to drive up here was Maynard's farm truck; dadgum thing hardly runs and tries my patience. Thank goodness Maynard's up the holler from our house at his Daddy's place today, cuttin' wood for their stove this winter, or we wouldn't have been able to git here at all. Lord knows Pearl wouldn't drive her good car up to my place. She was afraid it'd git mud on its tires."

"I was not, Garnet! Now, you don't start in on me again. I done told you I couldn't drive today because I feel a sick headache coming on."

"You's all the time feelin' something comin' on, Pearl. I'm surprised you ever popped out five younguns' between your headaches, your monthlies, and your weak nerves."

"Well, I never!"

"Well, if you did once in awhile, your might have a better disposition, and fewer headaches!"

"Girls," Ruby steps in, "Let's just head inside here, and git some lunch. Opal's stomach is a' growling. I just now heard it."

Good grief! I don't know what Ruby's got in store for us, but it better be good.

Garnet and Pearl git out of Maynard's truck, and head toward the house. I mosey on back into the kitchen, and start putting ice in the glasses for the soda pop Ruby brought.

"Garnet," Pearl continues her fussin' as they walk into the kitchen, "I don't know why you all the time have to be so unchristian. I have had trouble with my nerves, and you know my monthlies were always heavier than yours, but I've just done the best I can with what the Good Lord gave me. You might try calling on him once in awhile instead of taking his sweet name in vain. I heard you say it under your breath. Don't think I didn't." Pearl ends with a little sniffle.

"Dammit, Pearl! I swear I liked you a whole lot better before you got mixed up with Sister Deletha at the "Lord God Jesus is our Savior, just give us your money, and keep your doggone mouth shut Church!" It's hard to believe you're even one of us now. You're not any fun; in fact, you're just a prissy ole' goody two shoes that sucks the life outta anyplace where innocent people are trying to have a good time. If you want to know the truth, Sister Deletha is not the God-fearin' Christian she professes to be. Why, I remember her when they caught her in back of the tobacco warehouse checking out Kemper Steedman's crop! And I ain't talkin' tobaccer, either!"

"Oh, Heavenly Father," Pearl bows her head, and begins to pray, "Please rain your forgiveness down on Garnet, my earthly sister, for she knows not what she is saying. Please help her to . . ."

"Holy smokes, Pearl! We're not here to listen to your catterwawling! I want to know what's goin' on with sister Ruby. Plus, I'm ready to eat! Now, if you want to pray, bless the damn food, and let's git on with it!"

"Younguns, just cut out this foolishness," Ruby says, "Pearl, bless the food, and Garnet, just sit down before you have you one of them strokes like Ethel Ferguson did last year. She's still drooling all over herself in the nursing home and I don't think you want to end up like that. Bow your heads, girls. Now, pray, Pearl."

Pearl clears her throat and begins to pray.

"Holy Jesus, Sweet Son of God the Father Almighty, Savior of the wicked, Master of all that is good on this Earth and in the Heavens above . . . "

"Land sakes, Pearl," squawks Garnet, "Git on with it before the food gits cold and my disposition gits worse!"

"Pipe down, Garnet!" Ruby order, "Go on and finish, Pearl."

Being the oldest, Ruby always could git us in line almost as good as Mommy.

"Precious Lord," Pearl continues, "Just bless this food and help us to use the nourishment to your glory," she pauses, then adds hurriedly, "And please save Garnet's soul even though you know she don't deserve it! Amen."

"Pearl," Garnet starts.

"Girls, just cut it out right, now. For goodness sakes, let's just eat and git on with our visit." Ruby calls them into line again.

Goodness. I'm not sure what's going on with Ruby, but she must have something weighing heavy on her mind.

We finish up our lunch and take our coffee to the parlor. Ruby's brought one of her homemade red velvet cakes for us to eat while we have our visit.

"Girls, it sure does feel good to be here in Mommy's parlor," Ruby says.

"Yes, it does, Ruby," Garnet says, "but it still don't tell us why you've got us all up here today."

"Well, I reckon it don't. Girls," Ruby says as she leans forward in her chair, "I guess it don't take one of them rocket scientist to figure out Big Jim is a blowhard."

"Now, Ruby," starts Pearl, "He's your husband. Don't dishonor him."

"Hush your mouth Pearl," Garnet say, "Ruby's just speakin' the truth! We all know it!"

"Younguns, please let me git this all out. I . . . " Ruby voices quivers.

"Pearl, Garnet, let's allow Ruby to speak her piece. Can't you two quit your bickering for just a minute? Can't you see she's got somethin' mighty heavy weighin' on her?"

"Thank you, Opal," Ruby says as she begins to speak again, "Girls, when Mommy died last year, God rest her soul, it started me to thinking. I thought long and hard about growin' up here in this house, and how little we had to make do with when we was younguns. Mommy never complained, though. On the contrary, she seemed happy most of the time, except when daddy tracked coal dust through the house," Ruby chuckles.

"It occurred to me that my life was just the opposite of hers. I have all the material things I could want; I've got a good house, new furniture when I want it, and a new car to drive. Me and Big Jim's even got to travel a bit and see more of the country than Mommy and Daddy ever thought about seeing. It's just that there's something missin' in my life. It's that one thing Mommy and Daddy had that I've not had since the first few years I was married to Big Jim. You know what that is, girls?"

"I could venture a guess, Ruby, but I don't think you'd like my answer," pipes up Garnet.

Lordy sakes I'd better think of something quick. Heaven only knows what will come out of Garnet's mouth.

"Uh, Ruby," I say before Garnet can finish her thoughts on the subject, "Ruby, I'm just gonna go ahead and say this, and Lord knows I don't want to make you mad at me. You know I love you as only a sister could," I pause and catch my breath, "But, Ruby, I think the thing you're missing in your life is happiness, real happiness. Mommy and Daddy didn't have much to show for all those years of hard work, but they were happy. I hope I'm not bein' too pushy when I say that, Ruby."

"No, Opal, you're not." Ruby pauses a minute and her eyes start wellin' up with tears.

"Girls, I knowed all along Big Jim had a big mouth, and I thought I could live with that seein' how good he treated me otherwise. It's just, it's just . . . " Ruby's voice trails off.

"It's just you can't take his tomcatting around no more," Garnet blurts out, "There I've done gone and said it."

"Now, Garnet," Pearl chimes in, "Don't be goin' and disrespectin' Ruby's husband, too."

"No, Pearl," Ruby says, "Garnet's right. I'm just the last one in the county to acknowledge it. I never thought I hear myself say it out loud. Big Jim's been foolin' around since shortly after I got pregnant with Jimmy when we was first married. I've turned my head and closed my eyes 'til I just caint . . . "

Ruby's words end with a choked sob. I move over to where she sits on the couch. For once, we're all without words . . . even Garnet.

Ruby lays her head over on my shoulder and I hug her tight. I don't know what else to do. Garnet edges up off her seat to come over to where we are, then changes her mind and sits back down in her chair. Pearl bows her head and moves her lips. I make a silent prayer that she won't choose this time to preach one of Sister Deletha's sermons on adultery.

"Well, girls," Ruby says as she raises her head from my shoulder, and dabs at her eyes. "I guess you all know the truth, now. Funny, it don't seem as awful as I thought it would now that I've said it out loud."

"Ruby," Pearl says quietly.

"Pearl," Garnet squalls out at her, "Now, don't ya' start your preachin' . . ."

"Just a minute, Garnet Fergurson!" Pearl exclaims, "I reckon I know what to say to my own blood kin when I see they are a' sufferin'. Now just hold your horses and let me speak to my sister!"

We all git real quiet, real quick. I would've liked to snicker a bit, seein' as how Pearl put Garnet in her place, but I'm not sure I'd want to git drawn into one of their battles.

"Now, Ruby," Pearl continues, "I know you and my other two sisters think I don't have no mind of my own since I gave my soul completely to Jesus; but that's just not true. I know better than anybody what Big Jim's been doin' to you all these years. I seen him a' plenty of times stepping out with his hussies. I just figured it wasn't my place to come tell you. I knew you'd take care of it when the time come. Whatever you decide, you have my full support as your sister, and as a Christian woman washed in the blood of the Lamb."

"Well, wonders never cease! Pearl, you've got some sense of your own left in your noggin after all!" Garnet declares as she slaps her knee and lets out a cackle.

"I agree with Pearl," I say to Ruby.

Ruby looks around the room and musters up a smile for each of us.

"You younguns don't know what this means to me. Here's what I'm a' aimin' to do, if y'all back me up. I'm gonna leave Big Jim and move back here to the homeplace. You girls will have a place to come for Sunday dinner again, and when I'm gone, the three of you can fuss amongst yourselves about what you want to do with it. Right now, we all own it together. I just wanted to make sure it was all right with you if I's to move back in here, and set up housekeeping of my own."

We look at each other, all of us shaking our heads in agreement.

"Well, all right, then, girls, let's have us another piece of red velvet cake and celebrate comin' home!" Ruby says with a smile big enough to light up a country road after midnight.

We laugh and cry some more while we eat our cake; the four sisters from Jewel Holler, home once again.

About the Authors

Kori E. Frazier is completing her undergraduate degree in creative writing with a professional writing minor at Ohio Northern University in Ada, Ohio. Her poems have appeared in *Genie Magazine* and *North Central Review*, and she attended the West Virginia Writers Workshop in Morgantown, West Virginia during the summer of 2006.

Lisa Hall was inspired to write *Party Line* by her paternal grandmother who used her party line to stay abreast of events in her small Kentucky coal mining town. Hall recently had a personal essay published in the June issue of *Family Pastime Magazine* and is working on more projects. You may contact her at hall762@comcast.net.

Susan Noe Harmon, a native of Harlan County, Kentucky, has had her work published in the *Zephyrhills News*, Zephyrhills, Florida in 2005–06. In addition to co-founding a successful writer's group, her first novel *Weeping Willow Tales: Appalachian Memories* is nearing completion.

Susanna Holstein is a writer and performance storyteller. Her work has appeared in *More Teen Programs that Work* (Neal-Schuman, 2006), *Storytelling with Children* (NSN Press, 2005), *Mountain Messenger*, *WV Writers*, *Laurels*, and *BookPage*; she won five awards for poetry at the 2006 West Virginia Writers Conference. Susanna lives in Jackson County, West Virginia.

Pam Keaton is a member of the Society of Children's Book Writers and Illustrators and the Brown County Writer's Group in her home town of Mt. Orab, Ohio. She has recently finished her first mid-grade novel and is currently converting several of her short stories into children's books—including her own illustrations.

More information as well as samples of Pam's artwork can be found at www.pamkeaton.com.

Jennifer Poteet Mullins is a former third place winner in the Virginia Highlands Festival's Creative Writing Contest. Her short story "The Jungle Monster" took first place in the Lonesome Pine Short Story Contest in 2003. Also in 2003, she was awarded first place in the short story category, second place in the essay category and third place in the poetry category of Mountain Empire Community College's Art Competition. Her work has been published in *Writer's World Magazine*, *The Bristol Herald Courier*, and in Mountain Empire Community College's on-line magazine *Explorations*. Jennifer lives in Big Stone Gap, Virginia with her family.

Tricia Scott grew up in rural Ferrum, Virginia where she developed an affinity for superstitions and tall tales, morning glories, and a pan of good cornbread. Currently a home schooling mother residing in Roanoke, Virginia, Tricia is hard at work on a novel also set in the mountains of the Blue Ridge. She can be reached at triciascott@cox.net.

Tammy Robinson Smith published her first novel, *Emmybeth Speaks* (Mountain Girl Press), in 2005. The first chapter of the novel was awarded second place in the adult short story category at the 2003 Virginia Highlands Festival. After numerous years working as a broadcast reporter, then public relations professional, she founded Mountain Girl Press in 2005. Smith and her family reside in Bristol, Virginia. She may be contacted at publisher@mountaingirlpress.com.

Mary McMillan Terry is an adjunct professor of composition and American literature at Pellissippi State Technical Community College in Knoxville, TN. She grew up in the mountains of North Carolina and attended the University of North Carolina at Chapel Hill before moving to Knoxville for graduate studies. She enjoys teaching, writing, and research and has written an article on No Child Left Behind for a book on teaching, and entries for *The Continuum Encyclopedia of Young Adult Literature*.

Donna Akers Warmuth is a native of Washington County, Virginia. Her stories and poetry have been published in *Appalachian Heritage* and *Branches*. Warmuth's non-fiction articles have been published in *Smoky Mountain Living* magazine. Her work has placed in contests held by *Now & Then* and the Virginia Highlands Festival Creative Writing program. She has also contributed essays to the Morning Edition on WNCW in Spindale, North Carolina. Her published books include *Legends, Stories, and Ghostly Tales of Abingdon and Washington County, Virginia, Images of America: Abingdon, Virginia* (Arcadia Publishing), *Plumb Full of History A Story of Abingdon, Virginia* (High Country Publishers), *Boone, North Carolina* (Arcadia Publishing) and *Blowing Rock, North Carolina* (Arcadia Publishing). Contact her at 828-268-0970 or visit her website at www.donnawarmuth.com for more information.

Rebecca Lee Williams is a 4th generation descendent of Gate City, Virginia. Her current projects include writing screenplays and short stories. A locally recognized supporter of early childhood education and the Girl Scouts, she resides in Madison, Wisconsin with her husband, daughter, and two rambunctious terriers.

P. J. Wilson is an Appalachian writer living at the base of the Blue Ridge Mountains. She has the daily privilege of gazing at Terrapin Mountain to the south and No Business Mountain to the north. She has been published in a number of fine magazines and has written two young adult novels.

Tammy Wilson has lived more than half her life in North Carolina and has published dozens of stories in such journals as the *North Carolina Literary Review, The MacGuffin, Epiphany* and elsewhere. She was recently honored with a Virginia Center for the Creative Arts fellowship.

To learn more about Mountain Girl Press, or to order additional copies of *The Zinnia Tales*, go to http://www.mountaingirlpress.com. Bookstores and libraries may send inquiries to publisher@mountaingirlpress.com.

Also available from Mountain Girl Press

Emmybeth Speaks

Tammy Robinson Smith

Emmybeth Johnson is a nine year old girl who lives in Little Creek, Tennessee in the foothills of the Appalachian Mountains. Her story begins late in the summer of 1971. Emmybeth likes to know what is happening with the adults in her life and in the community in general.

She has a favorite "hidey hole" where she can listen as her mother, grandmother and the ladies from her church's sewing circle discuss the latest news and gossip from Little Creek. Emmybeth treats the reader to the "goings on" of the community from her naïve perspective, which is sometimes closer to the truth than she knows.

Emmybeth Speaks is a story about a community of women who band together to help a friend and her family in crisis. Emmybeth is a wonderful little witness and narrator for this phenomenon. It is her first brush with "Girl Power" and a lesson she won't ever forget.

Emmybeth loves her life in Little Creek and her family with all of her heart. She doesn't think her circumstances will ever change. When they do, the fallout confuses her but with the help of the women who surround her; she survives the change and endures. *Emmybeth Speaks* is a literary treat for all ages! Go to http://www.mountaingirlpress.com to order a signed copy today, or ask for a copy at your local bookstore.

Emmybeth Speaks
ISBN 978-0-9767793-0-8

Printed in the United States
200081BV00001B/241-297/A

9 780976 779315